D0199981

LOSERS
BRACKET

CHRIS CRUTCHER

LOSERS BRACKET

GREENWILLOW BOOKS
An Imprint of HarperCollinsPublishers

Losers Bracket
Copyright © 2018 by Chris Crutcher
First published in hardcover in 2018 by Greenwillow Books;
first paperback edition, 2019.

The text of this book is set in Maxime.
Book design by Sylvie Le Floc'h

33614081349242

Library of Congress Control Number: 2017957398

ISBN 978-0-06-222008-0 (pbk)

19 20 21 22 23 PC/LSCH 10 9 8 7 6 5 4 3 2 1

 Greenwillow Books

For all who have survived crazy families . . .
which is like, everybody

CHAPTER
ONE

The fact that life's not fair doesn't bother me. If the universe had distributed the IQ points allotted to my bio family evenly, we'd all dwell at the extreme low end of the range. But it made me "gifted" and the rest of them . . . not so much. That might sound like bragging but it's . . . yeah, bragging; but hey, this is *my* story. If they see it differently, let *them* tell it.

So, anyway . . . the universe also made me super coordinated and quick. Nobody in the rest of my family can juggle, like, *one ball*, though I have to leave open the possibility that Nancy—who contributed half my DNA—ate and drank and snorted away her athleticism. I hear my sis, Sheila, is a pretty good athlete in bed. Hard to believe we're sisters. My bio dad, Rance, is this ghost Nancy keeps at the edge of her life just so she can berate him.

I now live with another family altogether, which should be good news, but there's *something* about *real* family; you're connected, and that's it. Most times when I'm with Nancy or my sister Sheila, we fight like hungry pit bulls over table scraps, but when we're apart there's this crazy pull to get back, so historically I've done crazy stuff to make that happen. If the foster system really worked, it would have put Nancy with us in foster care. That way the person who needed help most would have gotten it.

But that didn't happen and Nancy lost three of us; there's an older brother, Luke, somewhere. Sheila was in and out like a ping-pong ball for most of her first ten years before social services stuck her in residential treatment. They took *me* before I dried off; no mother's milk for *this* future point guard, for which I should be grateful because God knows what all it would have been fortified with. *But,* no permanent home early on because if Nancy was better at anything than picking bad boyfriends, it was tricking social workers into thinking she was working on her "issues."

Service providers? I've known a few. Bet I could give you the first names of enough public health nurses to populate a softball team. FRS workers? Too many to name. FRS stands for Family Reconciliation Services. That's where your caseworker sends in a parent educator to help your mom deal with issues that arise when you've been sent back home for one more last chance. Issues like, should I duct tape my two-year-old daughter to the toilet seat in response to her shooting out nuclear *tag poop*. It's called that when you crap so much volume with so much force that it runs all the way up to the tag in the neck of your filthy Dora the Explorer T-shirt.

Issues like, can this nice man I met at a "cocktail lounge" last night live in the basement to help with rent? No? He *seems* nice. Is a level-three sex offender better or worse than a level-one sex offender? Doesn't matter? I promise I won't leave Annie alone with him.

So here I'd be, living with well-to-do people who provided for me and funded all my passions: youth basketball, parks and rec cross-country, and track. They kept me in the finest Nike gear and runners, gave me my own room with a walk-in closet and separate bathroom. And they bought me *books*. Then Nancy would save up enough drug money for some shyster lawyer to petition juvenile court to send me back for that one more last try and there I'd be again, in her three-room shack that smelled like the bottom of an ashtray, waiting every morning outside the one bathroom—while her new boyfriend sat on the throne reading the *entire* paper after he'd used all the hot water—so I could get in to run a comb through my ratty hair and brush my teeth, and then be late for school where my counselor could give me the third degree about why my attitude, and my appearance, had taken this unexpected downturn.

You don't tell her it's because you're back with your mom.

But here's the deal: if Nancy had been serious; if she'd stopped with the drugs and the creepy brand-new best friends, I'd have aired out that hovel and lived with her till I turned eighteen—wrapped myself in athletic gear from Play It Again Sports, walked to all my practices, and complained not a second. Because in the end, blood is thicker than good sense.

But the bouncing back and forth makes you crazy.

So what you do—or at least what *I* do—is figure a way to get as much bio-family time as possible while living in the lap of relative luxury. This does not necessarily sit well with your bios, because when you get together you're the one with the fancy clothes, the iPhone with the Bluetooth headphones, and the superior attitude.

It also grates on your foster family, because they notice a serious behavioral downturn after your day with anyone with the surname Boots. Pop Howard says it's like I've been hanging out so far up the holler I can't see the sun. In fact, once Nancy's parental rights were terminated, Pop put grave restrictions on my time with her and my evil sis. Like, none.

Which turned me into a liar.

For someone continuing to get the benefit of extreme doubt, Nancy was a master at getting on the bad side of social workers. See, if you choose the life of a social worker you're not going to make a lot of money, and people your age who majored in business and make four times your salary building websites and inventing software that lets you download free books and music snicker behind your back while they're telling you how much they admire your selflessness. Social workers don't so much get exasperated because five or six years of college has left them among the working poor, but if you don't cooperate with their do-gooding, it makes their career choice look ill-thought-out. At least that's the gospel according to my good friend and long-suffering caseworker, Mr. Novotny.

It was a whirlwind ending. I'm in fourth grade, nine years old, back at Nancy's because she peed clean for a month, which means she snuck somebody else's pee into the bottle. I'm trying to stay home from school to spend as much time with her as possible because this *never* lasts. I play sick but that doesn't work, because Nancy wants to look like a good parent and if I don't look sicker than she does when she's cold turkey, I'm not sick enough to stay home. I abandon that plan and tell her my teacher doesn't like me and lets the other kids bully me on purpose. Hey, I'm nine.

Next minute we're in the car headed for school, and from Nancy's raving I know I'm about to have some serious explaining to do. We shoot past the VISITORS PLEASE CHECK IN AT THE FRONT OFFICE sign so fast she couldn't possibly read it even if she could read, and head straight for my classroom, which I lead her to directly due to the pressure on the back of my neck. She kicks the door open so hard it breaks the doorstop and screams, "How dare you not like my Annie!" loud enough that three kids dive under their desks. "She's the sweetest girl in the world and she has a hard life! Her father is a no-good, two-timing drug dealer (like there are *good* two-timing drug dealers?) and her mother just ain't always done her best!" She jabs her thumb into her colossal chest.

Mrs. Granger puts a hand up to calm the kids, who stare at me like I just brought a giant python for show-and-tell, and walks calmly toward us.

"Get back!" Nancy says, raising an arm in defense. "I'll kick your ass!"

Mrs. Granger tells me to go to my desk and asks Nancy to step into the hall so they can discuss this away from her students.

"We'll discuss it right by-God *here*," Nancy bellows. I don't go to my desk because I can't break free.

"I like Annie just fine," Mrs. Granger says. "I like all my kids."

"That ain't what my Annie tells me an' my Annie don't lie!"

Mrs. Granger raises her eyebrows at me, because she's caught me in plenty of lies, and Nancy takes that as a sign she thinks I'm a devil child. "This little girl been through hell," she says. "She been left by her daddy and treated like a little piece of shit by me!"

Somebody laughs because we don't hear language like that in our classroom—from adults, anyway—but Nancy looks toward the sound like a pissed-off vampire and silence reigns.

Mrs. Granger tries to guide her gently into the hall, but that is not happening.

"Don't you *even* think yur gonna duck this humiliation, stickin' me out in the hall! I spent half my schoolin' in the hall!" Nancy's eyes narrow like a gunfighter's. "Raise yur hand if this woman don't like *you*, either."

No hands go up.

"RAISE YUR GODDAM HANDS!" and three shoot up involuntarily. I figure I am in about as much trouble as I can get into with this little effort.

Mrs. Granger quietly tells Nancy if she can't get herself under control, she'll have to call security, which has already heard the commotion and is on the way. Good luck. Two skinny security guys trying to get a five-foot five-inch, two-hundred-fifty-pound woman out a regular-sized door while she's grabbing desks and whiteboards and the globe, then going deadweight . . . again, not happening.

One of the guards is on loan from the city police force, so with help from the vice principal they're finally able to wrestle Nancy to a patrol car, and I am stuck with no credible explanation as to why my mother thinks my teacher doesn't like me. Luckily Mrs. Granger isn't like that and she just motions me toward my seat.

That was the end of the one-more-last-chances. Rance, my aforementioned sperm donor, hadn't participated in *any* services, so terminating on him was a no-brainer and by the end of the day I was back at the Howards' for good, oddly proud of my mother for her messed-up way of standing up for me.

June 29—Session #Who's Counting?
ANNIE BOOTS

Looking healthy in jock gear; got her basketball; mood seems fine. Got started a little late because of a crisis with the preceding client. Annie let me know right off she had to leave at the assigned time anyway. Typical Annie.

Annie: Nothing personal. I've got a shootaround with my Hoopfest team.

Me: Going up the losers bracket again, I assume.

Annie: (nods in the affirmative)

Me: Do your teammates know what's behind that?

Annie: Leah does. I tell Leah everything. The other girls don't need to know.

Me: You tell Leah everything? That's new.

Annie: Well, you know, everything you can tell out in the real world. I tell you everything.

Me: What do you want to talk about today? I'm assuming you don't want my take on your losers bracket one more time.

Annie: You are an astute assumer.

Me: So . . .

Annie: Do you remember the last time I got removed?

Me: Like it was yesterday. You broke a vase; said your removal was all my fault. Said your caseworker and I and all the teachers at your school made a secret plan to trick Nancy. Pretty rough language for a nine-year-old, if I remember.

Annie: Do you remember what really happened?

Me: I sure do. You lit your mother's fuse by lying about your teacher; thought you'd get to stay home from school, but instead of no people going to school, two people went to school.

Annie: Do you think it was my fault I got taken? Like if I hadn't said that about my teacher . . .

Me: I think it was your doing that you got taken on that particular day, but that incident was the very small straw that broke the camel's back. Nancy and Rance had already piled up an impressive stack. Why? What's bugging you? More dreams?

Annie: (big sigh) Yeah, I just keep seeing the look on Nancy's face when they told her at the next supervised visit that it was all over.

Me: I was told that "look" was a gunslinger's stare, followed by an impressive meltdown.

Annie: Yeah, but there was a second right before that. She was whipped.

Me: I don't know, Annie. You can see that look, you can dream that look, you can believe it was all on you. We both know how hard it is to outthink your feelings, but we also know there was no way Nancy was going to get it together to be your mom. You just got a bad draw, honey. What else you got?

Annie: You know, war with Pop.

Me: I thought we decided that's a battle, not a war. Come on, Annie, one year and you're on your own. Off to college, calling your own shots. Just hold it together.

Impression: Conflicted, which I see as normal for her age and time of life. The intensity comes from her history. Her swagger and trepidation will both get tested.

Emily Palmer, M.A.

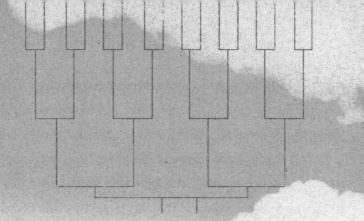

CHAPTER
TWO

So here comes summer between junior and senior year and Hannah, Mariah, and Leah (I know, a *lot* of *h*'s) and I are making our way through the massive Hoopfest crowd, looking for our court. Hoopfest is the largest three-on-three street b-ball tournament in the country. We've played together every year since we were ten and we've won our age group every time but once . . . when we came in second. After this year we go our separate ways.

Hannah and Leah are small and quick, I'm about middle, and Mariah *owns* the paint. You play three with one sub, so we can go big or small. A few other teams will give us a run, but in the end, we rule.

"Let's get through today undefeated," Leah says. "It's going to be in the high nineties, like our *shoes* could melt. We've had to come up through the losers bracket three years in a row." She frowns at me. Leah knows my "Losers Bracket" strategy and the reasons behind it, and she is not a fan, probably because we always win, but I seldom see any Boots. But she's my best friend, so most years she tolerates it; but it *is* hot. Leah's real sport is swimming—though it could be any sport she chooses—and Simone Manuel and Cullen Jones aside, she's well aware she could count the other top-notch black swimming studs on one partially amputated hand. Her plan, along with her younger sister, is to blow *that* trickle into a river.

"I know," Hannah says now, "we play three extra games when that happens; just one year I want to win straight through. We could die in this heat."

So we blow our first game on a missed short jumper by me, followed by shoddy defense. This girl I could spot ten points in a one-on-one game to eleven and beat ten times out of ten drives around me and lays one in to end it. She snags the ball as it comes through the net and flips it to me in a *take that* gesture that will cost her big when we see them again coming up through the losers bracket.

My teammates are scary quiet as we throw half-drunk

Gatorade bottles into our workout bags. Leah takes me aside and whispers, "*Un* means 'no'; *defeat* means 'loss.' What do you get when you put them together?"

I shrug. "Slow start."

"Uh-huh. Hoopfest has *emergency room* statistics about days like these."

"But think how much better we'll all feel when we come all the way back and win it," I say. "I mean, what feels better than, like, pressure?"

"Flu, acne, your period . . . "

"Okay, I get it."

She gives me her *look*.

Mariah squints and points at me. "You do know there's something wrong with you, right?"

I assure her I do.

Here's why the losers bracket. After the shoot-out between Nancy and Mrs. Granger, my hopscotching between homes was *done*. The Howards told Mr. Novotny they'd keep me until I was grown *if and only if* social services stopped bouncing me in and out like a bolo ball. They didn't adopt because that would have let the state off the hook if they decided to bail on me when I turned into Lizzie Borden at thirteen, which many experts told them was not only possible but likely. (I'm seventeen and it hasn't happened yet, but I'm not making any promises.) At any rate, they wrote up a long-term foster care agreement, which puts me permanently with the Howards until I'm eighteen, or until Pop Howard kills me.

So I didn't get the parents I want, but I got the ones I need. A childhood with the Boots does not lead one to Yale or Stanford or U-Dub or even Spokane Community. It leads to the corner of McDonald's and Walmart. Plus, certain times when Nancy and I get around each other, we fight from the time we're within earshot until one of us irritates the other so bad somebody uses the c-word; which is *crazy* because when I can't see her or Sheila or any of their lunatic entourage, I get really, *really* anxious. It's like when you go to IHOP and order the chocolate chip pancakes with Hershey's Syrup and a cup of hot cocoa; you know it's *bad* for you, but do you change your order to the omelet? You do not. So when I asked Mr. Novotny if we could have sporadic, supervised visits, he smiled, brushed his hands together, and said, "When your mom's rights were terminated, she became a *non*entity to me. *Non.* Over. Finished. *Done.* Free at last."

There's a restraining order on Nancy for the Howards' place because she has stalker in her DNA. Having Nancy lurking in a neighborhood like ours is like parking a rusted-out Chevy minivan on the Mercedes lot. It wouldn't be beyond her to threaten to kidnap Marvin, then hold a prisoner swap.

Marvin is the Howards' real kid, and though he has a *scary* IQ and vocabulary, he's not exactly what you'd call tough. Five minutes alone with Nancy and he wouldn't be able to put a sentence together.

The reason I know that particular threat isn't beyond her is, I've heard her make it.

After termination and the restraining order, no more supervised visits, so if I get to see Nancy or Sheila it has to be in public, where as long as one of them doesn't strap a bomb to herself, there's no keeping them away. Neither has thought of that yet. So at Hoopfest, the more games I play, the more chances I get to meet up. I hide these clandestine rendezvous from Pop Howard, because I live under threat of deportation. He's *invested* in me as a jock so he shows for most of my Hoopfest games and all my high school games, but he's got other business and stays only long enough to watch me play and tell me what I did wrong. He was, like, a third-string high school point guard on a state championship team, but when he tells it, "third-string" is conveniently missing. This might seem kind of mean, since the Howards have put up with my unpredictable behavior for eight years, but Pop is one of those guys who's way more interested in what he looks like than who he is.

At any rate, when Nancy does show she plays "Where's

Waldo?" in the crowd until he's gone. If you saw Nancy you'd recognize that as a difficult feat, but Pop is pretty self-absorbed, so he lays down his b-ball wisdom and splits.

By the time we work our way over to Hoopfest Central to see who we play next, my team has forgiven me our bogus loss and is ready to sweat it out back up through the losers bracket.

We could have won our second game with two players. There will be a few like that, but I have put the pressure on us to win them all. We towel off and Mariah and Hannah split in search of sno-cones while Leah meets up with her boyfriend to shoot over to one of the city pools to get in a few laps during noontime lap swim. She has the same passion for the pool that I have for the court. Tim Kim, the aforementioned boyfriend, thinks my losers bracket strategy is genius. Leah calls Tim her Korean breaststroker, which is interesting because he swims distance freestyle. Anyway, we all agree to meet fifteen minutes before our first afternoon game and I slip into Riverfront Park. If Nancy shows, she'll come through there.

"Well, well, if it isn't Cheryl Miller." My sister Sheila, parent of the year. She's with a woman I don't know, and Sheila's kid, Frankie, trails behind. Frankie's five.

"Hey, Sheila. Cheryl Miller's, like, fifty."

"Yeah," she says back. "I saw the end of your first game."

"You run into Nancy anywhere?"

She holds up a fist. "See any blood on my knuckles?" That means no.

I extend my hand to Sheila's friend. "I'm Annie. We're sisters."

"Yvonne." If her grip were limper, her hand would fall off.

"Half sisters," Sheila says.

I nod. "That's as much sister as you get in our family."

We exchange unpleasant pleasantries for a few minutes more before Sheila and Yvonne edge toward the street.

"Uh, what about Frankie?"

"Why don't you keep him for a while? Yvonne and I got business." I glance at Frankie, headed with his fists doubled toward a kid who's gotta be three inches taller and fifteen pounds heavier, and rush to grab him; at least if I've got him he won't show up on a milk carton.

"You gotta use your *words*," I tell him.

"Fuck you," he says.

"Different words."

"I hate you."

"Better."

I take his hand and we head for one of maybe twenty-five sno-cone stands.

My sister is not even two years older than me, but it feels like we were born on different planets. While I get it that I can be tough and unforgiving in a lot of circumstances, she is raw and rugged and dismissive in almost *all* circumstances. I know enough about *family* to have a pretty good idea what that means for Frankie.

We win our two afternoon games easily. Nancy never shows but her friend, Walter, does. I don't know the true nature of their relationship, but then I never do. He *is* way cooler than any of the others, even though he looks like he eats children. The guy is covered in reptilian tats, rides a hog, and carries a loaded pistol.

Walter says, "Something urgent came up."

"Was it in a pill bottle?"

He pats me on the shoulder, apologizes, and disappears into the crowd. I've got to do something about my quick temper; he didn't deserve that. Plus, I put a hurt on that second team all by myself, and just my luck, Momma and Pop Howard showed for it.

"You were rough on that girl," Pop said as I pulled my towel out of my duffel. I was sweating like a soaker hose.

"She could have called foul."

"Hard to call anything after a chop to the throat."

"No Nancy, huh?" Momma said. She's always suspected how I schedule my rendezvous.

"Don't know what you're talking about." I smiled when I said it.

Pop pushed my shoulder. "Well, if what-you-don't-know-what-she's-talking-about happens again tomorrow, remember it's Nancy you're mad at, not the girls on the other team. You embarrassed me."

I said it again: "She could have called foul." How did it embarrass *him*? All he's gotta say to explain me is, "She's a foster kid; there's something wrong with her." I sat, stretched my legs flat in front of me, and bent forward, forcing my head to my knees.

"If that had been a good team, they'd have wiped up the pavement with you because you wanted to hurt someone more than you wanted to win."

He was right, but I admit nothing to nobody.

Momma looked over at Frankie, who was being watched over during the game by Tim, who only thinks Frankie's pretty cool because he never spends long stretches of time with him. "No Nancy, but you did run into Sheila, huh?"

"Yeah."

"Frankie with us tonight?"

"That okay?"

She looked sideways at Pop, whose eyes were rolled so far back in his head he was staring at his brain. "Yeah, honey, that's okay."

"Sorry."

"I always wanted a big family."

Pop believes the more often we take Frankie, the more we tie ourselves to Sheila, and to Nancy by default. Hard to argue.

The Howards don't look like a Momma and Pop. They're, like, in their early forties and in killer shape. I don't call them Mom and Dad because that's what Marvin calls them, and it's only fair he gets first shot. He's their real kid, the un-jock. I picked "Momma" because there was this really cool black kid in fourth grade who called our teacher that—until he got suspended for calling our teacher that—and "Pop" covered the bases for his status and left "Dad" open in the unlikely event that mine comes out of his pharmaceutical coma.

Bringing a beastie like Frankie home—even for one night—should be against the law, especially into a home that includes a soft soul like Marvin. Marvin's already a little displaced by me because along with being a brainiac, he's artsy. Momma loves Marvin and his talents unconditionally, and maybe so does Pop, but you can tell he'd have rather had a boy he could play catch with, and maybe teach to shoot small forest animals. It's kind of a cliché that I'm the son he never had. Marvin gets even less attention when Frankie appears 'cause Frankie's a mean motor-scooter and a poop-grouter who has to be *watched*. Frankie will go *off* at the *smallest* slight or frustration, and as for the poop-grouting— *my* term—when he gets *seriously* off-center, he fills any small empty space with poop—his. He pushes it into the cracks in the walls in his bedroom, where regular grout is missing in the bathroom or shower, into cracks in tables or chairs or linoleum. You don't actually see him do it, you just find it. You smell it and you find it. There's no other way to say this: if Frankie's your foster kid, your house smells like shit. At first there's just a hint. *"Do you smell something?" "Does the house smell funny to you?"* Pretty soon there's nothing funny about the way your house smells. The trick is to keep him below that particular level of stress.

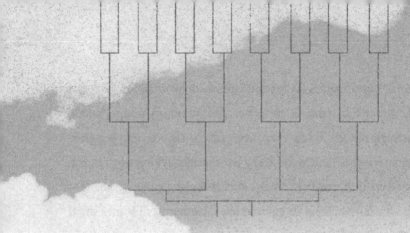

CHAPTER
THREE

I'm sitting on the curb pulling on my sweats after our title game. Hannah and Mariah have split, Leah and Tim are off with Frankie, buying him yet another sno-cone, Pop has deconstructed my play in maddening detail, and he and Momma are on their way to the car. Across the street Nancy stands beside Walter. I'd fire a hard one-handed pass straight at her smirky face, but I don't want to embarrass Walter any more than he *should* be embarrassed already. Look, if you're blessed with my mother's particular body design, do *not* wear tight shorts and body-hugging tank tops. And don't have an unlit cigarette hanging out of your mouth while clutching a King Kong–sized Big Gulp. Nancy's not morbidly obese, but she can be morbid.

We came back up through the losers bracket like always—beat that first team like a cheap bass drum on the way—and Nancy didn't see one game.

She's pointing her cinnamon bun at me, yapping ninety miles an hour into Walter's ear, so I know she's pushing him to come sell her excuses. Walter's resisting because it's gotta be a little humiliating to deliver the bilious dreck she wants him to convey, even though he knows I'll finally give him a pass because he's the most decent guy she's ever been with and we both know what a pain it is to talk her out of anything. *Bilious dreck*—how's *that* for advanced vocab? Marvin would be proud. Maybe I can find a place for it in my senior thesis.

Anyway, finally, he shrugs and saunters over.

I say, "Save it, Walter."

He nods. "Well, talk to me a minute, so it looks like I tried. You're going home to relative calm. I'm going . . . " He nods back toward Nancy.

I gaze into his earnest eyes. "You poor man. Why do you do it?"

"Your mom's not so bad," he says, "once you get used to her."

"I've known Nancy seventeen years. I don't recommend getting used to her."

"You act tougher than you are," he says. "Don't think I

don't know how the two of you sneak around. If you held her in the kind of disregard you claim, you wouldn't get so riled when she doesn't show."

As much as we do battle half the time, there's great relief knowing Nancy's finally with a guy she would never attack physically, and vice versa, and who would never steal her ill-gotten gains or live off her welfare.

Still, not that high a bar.

He says, "You've got to cut me some slack sometimes, like right now where I'm making it appear like I'm giving you her bullshit excuse. You *could* make it appear like you're buying it. Okay?"

I hear a combination of pleading and warning.

"So if you're gonna go over and have a conversation with her, just leave out the part where you're pissed. That'll make my day a whole lot easier."

Walter's as tough as he looks, maybe twenty or twenty-five years older than Nancy. Even though he stays over some nights, they don't live together because he doesn't want to mess up her "government wages" as she sarcastically calls what she gets for housing and disability and whatever else she can come up with to rob America's hardworking taxpayers. He works on motorcycles, washes dishes at a local sports bar, and sometimes works a third job, depending on scheduling. He keeps a one-room apartment five or six blocks from her place, a safe haven to which he can retreat when Nancy and Sheila go to war during one of Sheila's frequent visits.

I pat Walter on the back. "You do know," I whisper, "Nancy's not what most guys would call, like, a catch."

He gives me a hard glare. "People can't help how they look," he says.

Nancy stands on the sidewalk, a smile on her face, holding the Big Gulp in one hand and a Quik Mart cinnamon roll in the other. "Actually," I say, "to a certain extent . . . "

"You be kind. Under all that trouble, she looks a lot like you."

"Hey, Nancy!" I call to her.

She sets the giant plastic cup on the sidewalk, carefully removes the straw, balances the half-eaten cinnamon roll on the lid, and opens her arms as I cross the street to her. "Baby! You were great!"

"I was," I say, "but you only heard about it."

"I got here for the last game," she says. "You must not have seen me."

In deference to Walter I pass on the opportunity to tell her how impossible that would have been, but reflexively roll my eyes. Muscle memory.

"I meant to be here," she says.

I give in. "I know."

"Can we go somewhere?" she asks. "Walter, you'd buy us a late lunch, huh?"

"Gotta get," I say. "Momma's making celebration burgers for me and the team and . . . well, we've got Frankie."

"Where's Sheila?"

"Wherever Sheila goes."

"Want us to take him?" she says. "Social services doesn't need to know."

I shoot Walter a quick now-you-really-owe-me look. "Naw, we've got him."

"Baby, I really wish . . . "

"Nancy, if you want to spend time with me, make my games."

"There should be mandatory visitation," she says. "Them social service bastards."

"There *was* a visitation schedule. You made those less often than my games. And them social service bastards don't have anything to say about it anymore."

"Maybe so, but it's not fair. Your foster parents could . . . "

I punch her shoulder lightly. "Nancy. Come see me play." I nod to Walter. "You're free, friend. Go make memories."

Walter winks and gently takes Nancy's elbow.

"I feel for Frankie," Marvin says, "but, *whew!*"

"I know," I tell him, "but he'll only be here a little while, and if we stay vigilant, we can sidestep the olfactory assault."

It's past midnight. The team has been here, wolfed down some burgers, and split. I weathered Pop's repeated admonitions about letting my emotions affect my play, and now Marvin and I are digging in the fridge.

"Man," he says, "I still don't know how you survived your family."

"It's a wonder," I say. "But it's not as bad when you don't have to count on them."

"But you *did* have to count on them, I mean, back before."

I say, "According to my therapist, they counted on *me*. I was 'parentified.' And pretty much your parents saved me."

Marvin smiles. "You saved *me*. Every time you got sent back home, I'd *pray* your mom would screw up before my birthday. I'd put in my order for castanets or art supplies, and if you were still gone I'd get some kind of ball and a closet full of Adidas gear."

I glance through the kitchen doorway at Pop laying out the rules for Frankie. Along with all else, Frankie keeps outrageous hours.

"It's the curse of your gender."

Marvin's watching Pop, too. "He thinks I'm gay."

"I know. He asks me all the time. 'Does Marvin have a secret *friend?*'"

"Next time he irritates me, I'm gonna come out."

"You're not gay."

"I know," he says, "but I'll come out anyway."

"You think Pop doesn't like you."

"He likes *me*," Marvin says. "He doesn't like who I am. It should be the other way around."

"What's the difference?"

"If he liked who I am, you know, the things I really care about, he would automatically like *me*. But he has this utterly primitive idea of what a guy should be. He knows he can't change who I am and he's too thickheaded to know he'll be blown away by that someday. No lie, I'm gonna rock."

He will.

"*You're* the kid Dad always wanted," he says, "if you forget you're a girl. I love you like a *real* sister because when you're getting the lecture you just got, *I'm* not on the receiving end." He elbows me. "You just want to be sure he doesn't find about all the sneaking around."

Marvin's right. Pop knows I see Nancy at my games; he *doesn't* like it, but what can he do? He *doesn't* know how often I sneak to see Nancy or Sheila, or even Rance once in a while when I'm feeling sorry for him. I'm as two-faced with Pop as I am with them. It's not easy to be honest when nobody wants you to be doing what you're not going to stop doing. Momma knows way more than she lets on, but she *gets* it, so we have an unspoken deal.

It's only a couple of days before Sheila shows. I'm sitting on the front steps untying my shoes after a long, slow run when she steps out of the passenger's side of a Nissan pickup that looks like it should have machine guns in the back. Yvonne sits behind the wheel, cigarette dangling from her mouth, staring ahead.

Sheila looks a *little* contrite because even she knows it's not cool to leave your five-year-old for however long you want, with people who could report you with a phone call. But she also knows Momma and Pop want as little involvement with social services as possible. Momma says it's best to have a relationship with Sheila for Frankie's sake, and report only if things get dangerous. If we reported every time, he might bounce in and out like Sheila did all her life. Left to his own devices, Pop would put out a contract on anyone named Boots, figure some way to get Frankie into a loving home that isn't his, and be done with it. Truth is, if Frankie were here full-time, going head-to-head with Pop's controlling ways, he'd take a dump in Pop's sock drawer.

"Hey, hot stuff, is the rat still here?"

I say without looking up, "Did you call?"

"Yeah," Sheila says. "Jane said she'd have him ready."

"Then she probably does." I nod toward the front door.

Sheila hits the doorbell and I walk around back. I always feel bad and *really* angry when Frankie goes home with her, even though he's never here long before he goes psycho missing his mom. I know why, but that doesn't make me like it. It feels crazy to be attached to a kid with Frankie's unpredictable behavior, but he couldn't have been *born* that way. Sheila wasn't born the way she is, either, and when I remember that, I give her a break; if I'd gone into some of the foster families *she* went into, I'd be mowing people down in movie theaters by now.

July 6—Session #Who's Counting?
ANNIE BOOTS

Presents tan and healthy—bright shorts over a one-piece swimming suit, which means she's decided to repeat a behavior that didn't yield the best results, athletically, at this same time last year. This girl is a kick.

Me: Swimming again.

Annie: It's that time of year!

Me: If memory serves, your swimming should be done in water too shallow to actually swim in. On a towel. In the sand. Lots of sunscreen.

Annie: Funny. Swimming's good for me. It uses completely different muscles.

Me: Which, if that were your goal, would be good.

Annie: Don't know what you're talking about. (she's being sarcastic)

Me: Uh-huh. Annie, since I started working with you, at age nine, you've been doing this thing I call oddball sports. You did soccer—that one made some sense, athletically—field hockey, not so much; lacrosse, where you almost killed a girl; cross-country . . .

Annie: Don't forget curling.

Me: (cannot prevent my own teenage eye roll) Right. Curling. And no matter if you had to win to play more games, or lose to play more games, how many contests have your mother or Sheila or your father attended?

Annie: (big sigh) You think there's something wrong with me?

Me: You are in a therapist's office once a week. (gets me a laugh) What's bringing this all up again? Maybe that's what we should be looking at. We've agreed your responses are . . . a little bizarre . . . but over the years they come and go. What's going on now?

Annie: I'm not sure. I have some of those dreams, or flashbacks or whatever; you know, where Rance has come out of his coma and is threatening everyone; Nancy grabs the bread knife. Sheila jumps in on one side or the other and I just stand there. I know I'm supposed to do something, but my feet are stuck and I'm yelling but no sound comes out.

Me: And when do you get those dreams?

Annie: I know, I know. When I haven't seen anybody, so I don't know if everyone's all right.

Me: And when you do see somebody and figure out everyone is all right . . . relatively speaking . . . what happens?

Annie: I fight with them.

Me: Because . . .

Annie: I'm mad that they made me worry.

Me: And . . .

Annie: I know, I know. I hate that they're okay without me.

Me: And . . .

Annie: That they don't need me.

Me: And . . .

Annie: They don't want me. (tears well; but she's showing me the tough Annie, willing them back)

We sit quietly. In one form or another this is a repeat, but naming it usually relieves pressure.

Me: It's circular. You engage in behavior that yields little, and the less it yields the harder you try.

Annie: The definition of crazy, right?

Me: The definition of spinning wheels. So what are you going to do about this swimming thing?

Annie: (stands, pops her forehead with the palm of her hand) Workouts start tomorrow noon.

Me: Bye, Annie.

Annie: Same time next week?

Me: Same time next week.

Impression: Coming into her last year of high school, then headed into truly uncharted territory. Her trepidation clashes with her need for control. Not unusual given her history, but could be in for a rough patch.

Emily Palmer, M.A.

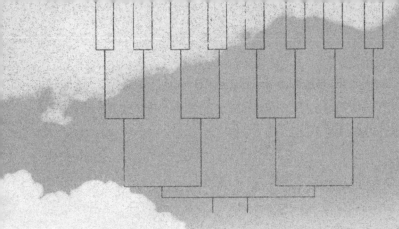

CHAPTER
FOUR

With Hoopfest behind me, I'm headed for uncharted waters. Literally. I could play AAU basketball for the rest of the summer, but I'd be on an elite team, which would mean games out of town pretty much every weekend, which would leave me a lot fewer chances to hook up with my roots. Tomorrow I hit the water.

Lesson in relativity: To gauge my success in basketball I consider points, assists, percentages of field goals and foul shots made, rebounds, and fouls. In swimming it's fear on the face of the lifeguard.

This is Leah, talking me into turning out the first time: "You practice every day, so if anybody from your crazy family wants to be there to claim your body when you drown, they can. You'll never make the A team—*my* team—we have an out-of-town meet every week. You'll be stuck right here in the city park, swimming with the *suck* team."

"How can I refuse?"

She holds up a finger; there's more. "If you qualify in the prelims of an event, you swim later in the finals. So pick events nobody likes to swim. Like the fifty fly or one hundred I.M. Almost nobody on the suck teams can do all four strokes, so all you have to do to place is not get disqualified. I can help you with that."

"What's an 'I am'? I am what?"

Heel of the hand to the forehead. "I-period, M-period," she says. "Individual medley."

"Which doesn't increase my fund of knowledge one bit."

"Twenty-five yards of each stroke," she says. "It's awful for beginners. Sometimes you'll be in the water alone. Finish alive, you get a blue ribbon."

I don't mind hard work. I don't even mind turning out for a sport at which I know I'll be abysmal, but the universe did not engineer my body for the butterfly.

"Doesn't have to be pretty," Leah says when I tell her that. "Just legal. *Plus,* you get to dazzle some young horny Michael Phelps never-be studs laying out on a blanket in your skimpy

Speedo two-piece between races. They'll come around telling you what a good race you swam or asking if you saw theirs, and since you're *completely* uninterested you'll tell them how good they looked and give them that smile you give that you know will drive them crazy."

"What smile . . . "

"I've seen you at work, girl. You aren't *me* in that suit, but you're the next best thing."

There *is* something powerful about making guys drool, even if they're doughy little boys three to six years younger, walking around between races with their beach towels high up under their boy boobs to hide their cottage cheese love handles. I'm pretty sure this sick little part of me has something to do with what Nancy calls my "Boots wiring," which is designed to "git yourself a man."

Our coach, though, presents a greater challenge. This guy turns heads. He's a student at Whitworth University, probably the best swimmer in our region, if you don't count Leah, and dead serious about this swimming thing. He's built like a *real* swimmer, and it's a challenge to make him look at me the same way the little boys do. His name is Rick Sebring, and if there's a straighter arrow anywhere, it's gotta be his girlfriend, Janine, also a Whitworth swimmer and Rick's assistant coach. She's really nice and really patient and every bit as pretty as she is tough, or vice versa, which kind of makes me jealous.

I'm not really trying to take Rick from Janine. In fact, I know from a couple of bad junior high experiences that "Boots wiring" is just another term for "trouble." I was a victim of "early development," and Nancy told me every chance she got that "them titties" could get me all of what I needed and most of what I wanted. I'm not going into it, but mostly they got me fingerprints and lies. So even though it would be easy to travel that road, I am *not* going down it. I never go out with a guy more than three times, and only then if he keeps his hands in his pockets. But I have an overdeveloped yearning to be wanted, which doesn't speak highly of me, and I *do* like making another girl nervous.

So I'm walking out of the dressing room at Witter pool, net bag slung over my shoulder with my wet Speedo, swim cap, and goggles inside, scanning the parking lot in case there's a misplaced Boot hanging around.

"Annie, hey!" Rick. Coach.

"Yeah?"

"Got a minute?" Janine is headed toward his car.

"Yeah."

He catches up to me. "Listen, what are your goals?"

"*Dancing With the Stars*," I say. "My own reality show."

Slight grimace. "For swimming."

"Stay on top of the water; move toward the far end. Repeat."

"Didn't I see your name in the *Review* for winning your division at Hoopfest?"

"Yeah."

"And weren't you All-City last year?"

"Second string," I say.

"So what are you doing in the water?"

"Staying in shape?" I give him a look.

"You put that as a question. Why aren't you on an elite summer basketball team?"

"I like to try new stuff. Is that okay?"

He shrugs. "It's okay by me, but I'm going to be cranking up the yardage once some of these younger kids look like they can take it. Coach Cole is looking for the studs who can move up. Your stroke isn't exactly . . . "

"Olympic?"

"I almost jumped in to pull you out twice today."

I murmur. "That's good to know."

He frowns. "What?"

"I'm in less danger than I look. Don't worry, I'll get the hang of it and I'll put in the yards."

"Long as you know what you're getting into."

Janine hollers from the car, "Hey, sweetie. You coming?"

He turns and jogs away. They talk for a minute before he starts the engine, while I convince myself I caused a little trouble.

Marvin meets me at the door. "Man, am I glad to see you."

"What's up?"

"Frankie's up."

"He's back already?"

He nods. "And Sheila looked quite roughed up." What seventh grader says "quite roughed up"? I never *quite* get used to Marvin. He dresses like a kid—sandals and baggy shorts and T-shirts, though his T-shirts are often telltale. Today's says, "There is a reason for everything, and that reason is science."

"How bad?"

"Facial bruising, swollen lip; you know . . . "

Sheila does like the bad guys. "But Frankie's okay?"

"*Relatively*," he says, and smiles. "I mean, he's still *Frankie*."

"Is he doing his Frankie *thing*?"

"Uh-uh, but only because I'm following him like a secret service guy. Man, I don't get it. How come it doesn't bother *him* as much as me?"

I shrug, punch his shoulder. "Frankie runs on negative

feedback. You look like you've had enough. Where is he?"

"In the bathroom." He points to the closed door. "At least he's close to where he *should* be putting it."

"Never let him close the door," I tell him, and bang on the bathroom door. "Frankie, open up!"

Silence.

"Frankie!"

Nothing.

"You better not be doing what I think you're doing!"

From behind the locked door: "I not."

"Yeah, well, you were thinking about it."

Silence. Then, "How come you know?"

"I know everything. Open up. If I have to jimmy this door, you're *really* in trouble."

Laughter.

I say, "You're gonna think funny."

"Jimmy," he says, and laughs again.

"It means 'break in,' Frankie. Open the door."

"I don't like bosses," he says. "If I open this, you don't be mean to me."

"I don't like bosses, either," I say. "If you open it, I don't be mean to you. If you *don't* open it, I do be mean to you."

Silence.

"Frankie?"

Nothing.

"If you're smearing . . . if you're doing the *bad* thing, I'm going to tie you to your bed."

"That's mean!"

Uh! "You're right. If you're doing that, you and I are going to get a rag and some soap and scrub everything till it smells like roses."

"Not smearin' nothin'."

"Good. Then we can go play. Open up." No wonder Sheila dumps this little Martian off so often; he's exhausting.

I hear water running. "Frankie, will you open this door? Please?"

"I might take a bath."

"You can take a bath if you want, but you gotta open the door first."

"I just like bosses what don't boss me," he says. "My teacher bosses me but I just don't do what her say. Her gets mad."

"I'm not your teacher, Frankie. Neither is Marvin. Open the door and we promise we won't boss you."

"Marvin bosses me."

Marvin is shaking his head. He whispers, "I will *vacate*."

"Marvin won't boss you."

"He say I drivin' him crazy," Frankie says.

Marvin's nod affirms it. "That's why he won't boss you. He doesn't want to be crazy. Frankie, Open. The. Door."

After a brief silence the knob clicks. I wait for him to come out.

Marvin smiles, puts both hands in the air. "See, buddy? No boss here. I'm leavin' you with the Goddess of All Things Strange."

Frankie says, "See ya."

Marvin whispers as he passes, "Dismissive little shit."

"So, wanna go play?"

"Uh-huh," Frankie says.

"Inside or out?"

He looks through the window. Bright and sunny. Warm. "In," he says.

I say, "Out."

He wrinkles his nose.

"Go downstairs and grab some trucks and a couple of superheroes. Get the bucket and the shovel." We're only a few minutes from Manito Park playground. There's sand there. Swings. A little water park. "Get your suit." As often as Frankie shows up here without notice, Momma keeps an "emergency Frankie drawer" full of clothes and toys, etc. He comes up in shorts and a long-sleeved shirt that looks way too hot to me.

"No suit," he says. "No water."

"Bring it anyway. We don't have to use it."

At the sandbox at the park I snatch Frankie by the back of his shirt as he tries to take another kid out for messing in *his* sand and getting close to *his* trucks, and plop him in a corner facing away from all possible combatants. He plants a super villain figure upright in the sand, crashes into him from behind with a dump truck. "Fuck it for you, Butch!" he yells, and runs him over again.

"You gotta *whisper* that word," I tell him.

He crushes Butch once again and in a very loud whisper, says, "Fuck it for you, Butch." He hides "Butch" behind a sandy mound, but the dump truck plows through and mows him down.

"Is Butch *real* or pretend?"

Frankie glares, brings a foot down on Butch.

"Frankie, who's Butch?"

He seems not to hear.

"He a boss?"

"Not *my* boss," he says, stomping Butch. "I kill him."

"You don't like bosses."

"Nobody's the boss of me. I be my own boss." *Stomp!*

"Is Butch at your mom's place?"

He looks away.

"Does he live at your house, Frankie?"

"He's not the boss of me!" Frankie yells, and jumps up and down on Butch's sandy grave.

I flash on the fights that have turned physical in *my* life, shake it off, and nod toward the water station, where kids splash, man the rotating water machine gun, stand under revolving, randomly tipping buckets of water. "Hey, guy, I'm hot. Let's get wet."

He absently touches the upper arm of his shirt. "Huh-uh. Too cold."

"Frankie, it's ninety-five degrees out here."

"NO!"

"YES!" and I wrestle him into the sand, bounce up, and crouch into a wrestler's stance.

Frankie charges and crashes against my leg, and I let him pull me down.

"Great tackle! You'll be drafted out of grade school."

I'm on my back, Frankie straddling my chest, fist cocked. I catch his arm mid-swing. "Illegal use of the hand! Come on, buddy, you can't play like that. Somebody gets hurt."

He swings with the other arm. I block it, jump up, and haul him toward the water. Frankie squeals in fake protest, obviously forgetting his aversion to cool water in ninety-five degrees. In seconds we're standing beneath a bucket, soaked to the bone. I run to the mounted water machine gun, swing it around, and fire; Frankie drops to his belly, crawling like a soldier through the stream yelling soldier threats. I throw off my soaked outer shirt and kick it out of the way. Frankie does the same, and I cease fire.

Frankie yells, "Keep shootin'!"

I drop to a knee, take his arm. A dark bruise over swelling covers his entire biceps. He tries to cover it.

"Lemme see."

"I forgot," Frankie says, staring at his arm. "I done it. I falled down. It wasn't Butch. It doesn't even hurt."

I touch the wound and he flinches.

"Is this why you were driving Butch into the ground with your truck, Frankie?"

"Butch don't hurt nobody," Frankie says. "Him a good guy."

"Who told you that?"

"Butch."

"Frankie, how did this happen?"

"We was tradin' punches."

I close my hand gently over the bruise. "Come on, bud. Let's go back. You can watch a show."

"That didn't take long," Marvin says as Frankie scurries up the front walk.

"Breaking news," I say. "Sheila's not the only one scuffed

up." I don't explain, and instead ask Momma if it's okay to take the car, then hurry into my room to grab my cell.

Me: *Sheila's address*

Nancy: *Who wonts to no*

Me: *I wonts to no. Give me the goddam address*

Nancy: *Don't be snoty*

Me: *Sorry. Give me the address please*

Sheila's address pops up on my screen.

"Hey, Sheila." I stand on the porch staring at her through the broken screen. She does look rough—bruised cheek and swollen lip, dirty jeans with a hole in the knee that she didn't buy to look that way, ratty blouse that I recognize came from Nancy.

"How'd you find me?"

"Siri."

"Who the fuck's Siri? What are you doing here; is Frankie okay?"

"Depends on what you mean."

"I mean is he still at your place?" She looks at the ground.

"Yes."

"So why are you here?"

"Somebody here named Butch?"

"No."

"You lying?"

"Shut up, bitch. I said no. He's not here."

She didn't say she doesn't *know* Butch. "Where is he?"

"Thanks to *Frankie*, gone."

"What did Frankie do?"

Her eyes narrow. "He didn't do nothin', that's what. Nothin' Butch told him."

"Right, so Frankie wouldn't behave and Butch put bruises on him." It kills me that Sheila can't remember what it was like to have some new guy show up and take the reins when he had never learned to ride, guys who thought that nothing but *time* on the planet qualified them to be the boss.

"Frankie hit 'im," she says, "so Butch hit 'im back. Told Frankie to take his best shot."

"Trading punches." Jesus.

"Frankie's gotta learn not to hit. Butch was just teachin' him. . . . "

"Not to hit by hitting him."

"He was showing him how it felt, you dumb bitch!" You can tell when Sheila knows she messed up; she defends herself by attacking.

"Sheila, how much therapy have we had? Between the two of us?"

"Fuck therapy."

I start to tell her she had to learn *some* basics, but this is about to go off the rails.

"You don't have to worry, anyway," she says. "Butch is gone. For good."

"Yvonne here?" I ask.

"She got pissed an' left."

"She gone for good, too?"

"No! For now. What the hell, she has her own place. That's none of your goddamn business anyway."

"I was just asking if you were alone."

"Damn right I'm alone. Kid like Frankie, how am I gonna be any other way?"

I shrug. "You told me Yvonne stays here as much as her place."

"Yvonne thinks I can't keep a man 'cause down deep I'm a dyke, like her. That's why she's here so much—thinks she can *rescue* me." She snorts.

I'm thinking, *That would be good all the way around,* but I don't say it. "Let's get a pizza."

"Where am I gonna get money for a pizza? Butch took . . . "

"I've got money."

"Why you bein' nice? You come over here to jump my shit about Frankie, and don't say you didn't."

I raise my hands. "No reason I can't jump your shit over a pizza."

She looks back into the dark house. "Well, the TV's busted. . . . "

"Okay then."

We're sitting on the floor next to a coffee table crafted from two cardboard boxes holding up an old door, killing off four meats with extra cheese.

"So go ahead," Sheila says. "Jump my shit."

I scan the dingy room. "How is anything ever going to be different, Sheila? I mean, you keep Frankie out of foster care by leaving him with us, but it's drugs and people like this Butch guy and pulling it together long enough to take him back, and then . . . well, all over again."

She takes a bite of pizza, wipes her mouth with the back of her hand, looks at me hard. "You wouldn't get it."

"I'll try. I will."

She stares at me a bit longer. "Naw, fuck it. Doesn't matter whether you'd understand or not. You're right; nothin's changin'. You wanna know what it's like to be Sheila Boots? I got two gears, Annie. Either I'm either up in somebody's face gettin' ready to beat the shit out of them or getting them to beat the shit out of me, *or* I'm lookin' for a way out."

"A way out?"

"You remember that chick that loaded the kids in the car and took 'em into the lake? Susan somebody?"

"Smith," I say. "Susan Smith."

"Yeah, her. I'm not sayin' I'd ever do that, but I sure as hell know why she did."

My heart pounds. "You're not . . . "

"No, I'm not gonna off the little shit an' I'm not gonna off myself. I got too many people I want to piss off. And don't you go runnin' to your fancy foster folks, or your fuckin' caseworker, sayin' I'm over the edge, because I'm not."

I can feel her retreating into her armor. "You remember that time when I was in, maybe, third grade, and Nancy took me 'shopping'?"

"I remember a lot of times like that."

"Well," I say, "this time, the store guy caught us and was going to call the cops?"

"Yup."

"Nancy talked him out of it?"

She nods.

"You remember what you said to me when we got back and Nancy was bragging about how she made the 'old fool' feel sorry for us, and I was laughing?"

"What'd I say?" Sheila looks bored.

"You took me out back and threatened me—said no matter what happened, no matter how many fosters we got stuck in or whatever, if I turned out like Nancy you would kick my ass."

"And I would've, too."

"Sheila," I say, "you're turning out like Nancy."

She swipes her hand across the coffee table, sending meat and cheese and crust flying. "I can still kick your ass," she says, and our sisterly connection *vanishes*.

I jump up; you do not want to be caught already down when Sheila comes after you. "It's been a while since you've tried," I say, and she takes it exactly how I meant it, rises slowly, fists doubled.

"It wouldn't piss you off so much if it wasn't true," I say, backing toward the door. I don't know if she can take me or not. I'm in a lot better shape, and pretty tough as midsized chicks my age go, but I've seen my sister in fights before and she never stops getting up.

She says, "Looks like this party is over."

And that ends that.

July 20—Session #Who's Counting?
ANNIE BOOTS

Came in with purpose today; not always the case. Intensity apparent in body language; marched in, sat, leaned forward, foot tapping, fingers drumming.

Me: What's up?

Annie: Tell me again about Sheila. Me and Sheila.

Me: What can I tell you that you don't already know? Did something happen?

Annie: Kind of the same thing that always happens. I get with my sister and things are going relatively well—we're kind of understanding each other and then BLAM! It always ends in BLAM!

Me: That's been going on as long as you've been seeing me. Why was this time different?

Annie: It's not different, that's the problem. When Sheila gets mad it's just . . . exactly what I expect. No big deal there. What I hate is, that later it makes me crazy when I want her to . . . want me; you know, listen to me.

Me: Remember, we've been here before, Annie. It's always going to be a struggle for you when what makes sense won't settle in your stomach . . . or your heart.

Annie: So what do I do?

Me: What can you do?

Note: The rest of the session was spent on the struggle Annie will face all her life—the struggle between her brain and the hard wiring of her heart. If there is a takeaway, it's this:

Annie: You told me once you went through some of the things I'm going through.

Me: I did tell you that.

Annie: How did you, like, survive?

Me: Truth? I got older. I got older and I got smarter. The feeling doesn't go away, but it gets more recognizable, and I've learned to see it coming. It gets better, Annie.

Annie: It better get better.

Me: But you can't just wait for that.

Annie: I know, I know. I gotta make it.

Emily Palmer, M.A.

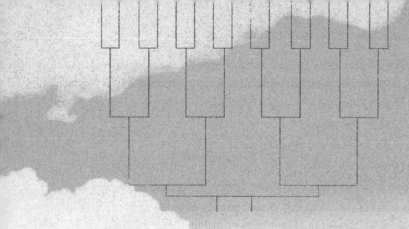

CHAPTER
FIVE

The uncool thing about swimming is I suck *so* bad the workouts are at least as torturous as I feared when Coach Rick said he'd be cranking up the yards. It's possible Janine, kind, patient girl that she is, doesn't like the way I twitch my bikini butt at her boyfriend, because she's decided I should be a butterflyer and has taken me on as a project; "helping" me with my stroke when my arms are so heavy I can't get them out of the water to hoist up some sign language. Leah warned me about messing with her.

"Your arms aren't clearing the surface after the first two strokes," she says. "You look like a sinking windmill. Work on shoulder flexibility." Quiet, calm voice. Instructional. Instructions my body is not built to follow. "You'll get it," she says, and pats my wet head. "Never give up."

Go help someone who can swim. I canvass beyond the chain-link fence for Nancy.

"We work out every day at noon," I told Nancy after I signed up. "Just come down once a week. Bring Sheila; she'll *love* how I suck. I'll buy you lunch."

It *doesn't* make sense that I care so much, but my heart goes back to those days when I was five and it was just the three of us in a hollowed-out single-wide, days when I would have done *anything* to make her, or Sheila, proud, make them want me.

"I'll be there every day, baby," she said four weeks ago when I made the change between my best sport and my worst. She's showed up *once* so far, waited outside the pool area long enough to say, "You're not very good at that. Them other kids're swimmin' right on past you."

I should have known that if Nancy had only made a small fraction of my b-ball games, she sure wasn't going to make *practices*.

"Well, I enjoyed it. Keep it up. I'm meetin' Walter." That was our visit. My brain is wired *backward*. The minute she does show I'm ready for a fight, but when she *doesn't* I get this . . . *emptiness*. It's like those chicks who cut on themselves; no obvious upside, but every one of them says there's *relief* when the blade or the piece of glass slices through.

Today as I'm walking out of the dressing room I overhear Janine talking to Coach Rick: "I think Annie should swim fly in the relay, too." *That's* a mean girl.

"Serious?" Rick says. "She looks kind of desperate in the water."

"I know," Janine says. "But she'll *do* it."

So now I'm the butterflyer in the fifty *and* the relay, which will teach me great humility.

Our first meet is scheduled for late afternoon Wednesday at our pool, where we'll swim against the suck teams from the other city pools. A-team meets have ticket prices and concessions and portable bleachers where swimmers' parents sit on padded benches under a canvas overhang that shades them from the hot summer sun. Wipe *that* out of your head. Three wooden benches stand on the grass outside the pool, occupied mostly with homeless guys who heard the starting gun and came over to see if someone got whacked, or who saw the backstroke flags being strung and thought the carnival was in town.

The meet is scored as five separate dual meets—each team swims separately against each of the others—so I can actually finish dead last and still get points against teams who don't have anyone dumb enough to swim fly, or flyers with my same crappy stroke but less tenacity. This is my first formal competition, and though I have *no* identity tied up in being a swimmer, the anticipation of competition and the fear of looking like someone has thrown a cat into the pool, has my stomach dancing.

The longest race for the younger kids is just twenty-five yards, and even *I* could navigate that, but my age group goes fifty—up and back—and I might as well be swimming the English Channel with an anvil tied around my neck. I thought I had it down, but adrenaline has leaked into my brain and washed out all Janine has taught me; the starting gun fires and three strokes into the race I'm cursing Janine like she's the Antichrist. Three-quarters through the first lap I meet the first swimmer on her way back. Coming back I look like the person hired to pretend she's drowning on the final day of Red Cross senior lifesaving class, and five feet from the finish my feet drag on the pool bottom. *That* would get me disqualified in the Special Olympics, and it does so here; basically I find a way to *not* earn points while still finishing dead last.

Janine stands beside the judge as he writes out my disqualification slip. "Don't sweat it," she says. "You've still got the relay."

"You're not really proficient, are you?" Marvin greets me as I exit the locker room.

"What are you doing here?"

"You know, scouting the town for comedy. Any Boots on the ground?"

"If anybody showed, they were so embarrassed they left before they had to talk to me."

Marvin giggles.

"What?"

"Just picturing things that might embarrass your family."

We walk toward the bike rack; I could have come in the car but Spokane is getting better and better with bike lanes. One thing about living here: people like to be in shape.

"Go out for AAU track." he says. "At least there's *air*."

"I'm too fast," I tell him. "I'd be on the traveling team the first week."

"Sign up for something you suck at. Shot put, maybe."

It's a thought, but probably a bad idea to put into my hands a weapon I could drop on Nancy's foot.

"You know," he says, "you could make yourself sick doing what you're doing."

"Don't start."

"Just sayin'."

"Stop sayin'."

I peel off at the entrance to the parking lot of our branch library. "Come on in," I tell him. It's an hour till book club. I'll buy you a pop."

"This is as far as I go," Marvin says. "My library's in my room—comes complete with keyboard."

Marvin rides on while I chain up my bike.

So I'm standing in the middle of the main room, deciding how to kill the hour, when I hear, "Hey, girl."

I turn around. "Walter! What are you doing here? Is Nancy . . . "

He snorts. "You think it's unusual running into *me* in the library. . . . "

"Yeah, what was I thinking?"

He waves his hand in a wide circle. "My sanctuary," he says. "Come here to get away. . . . "

"From Nancy?"

He smiles. "From everything. But you're right, she'd never look for me here. I tell her I'm going to the Corner to play some cards."

"I've got a mother who'd rather have her boyfriend in a bar than a library."

"Your momma doesn't want me getting too smart."

"How would she know?"

"Stop it. You gotta give her a break ever so often."

"Every so often I do."

"You here for your book club?"

"I am."

He looks me over, closes one eye. "You don't always strike me as the literary type."

"It's not like we read Shakespeare," I say.

"Oh yeah? What dost thou read?"

"Lotta stuff—stuff that's recommended by other kids, or that's just popular. Sometimes it's fiction, sometimes real stuff—nonfiction—that just makes us smarter about the world; you know, events that a lot of people don't know about or just about unusual people. Like big guys with small brains who cover themselves in tats and ride Harleys."

"So," he says, "like *real* heroes."

"Yeah, like that."

"You're a funny girl."

"So," I say, "we both like books."

He nods toward a couple of overstuffed chairs, so I follow him over, where he sits. "Naw," he says. "You like books. I *love* books."

I sit, too. Walter's been around off and on for a long time, though in different capacities at different times. He knew Nancy and Rance back in their major drug days, and he's way older than they are. But in recent times, he's been the only guy I've seen Nancy with. Their relationship has changed, though I'm not sure exactly how.

"Does Nancy know this about you?" I ask. "Your thing with books?"

"What possible good would *that* serve?" he says.

"What kind of stuff do *you* read?"

He glances around the cavernous room, waves a hand over it all. "Perty much anything," he says. "Ever'thing. Didn't get a chance to finish college but hey, almost any book you'd find at a university is one you can find here."

"You went to college?"

"Don't look so surprised. When you get there, look around. There'll be plenty of scurrilous dudes."

"How come you didn't finish?"

"War."

"Really? Which one, like, World War Two?"

He laughs. "How are you at math?"

"I get by. Cheat when I have to. Why?"

"Bet you cheat a lot. If I'd fought in World War Two, I'd be in my nineties. I get that I haven't kept myself up, but I sure as *hell* don't look ninety. It was Vietnam. 'Nuff said."

What I get is the "'nuff said." Walter's an enormous man who you wouldn't want to meet in a dark alley, but if there's a side of him that's like that, I've never seen it. However, it's pretty clear he doesn't want to talk about the war, and "'nuff said" is all I need to let it drop.

CHAPTER
SIX

The book club is a different world for me—different from my Hatfield-and-McCoy existence with the Howards and the Boots, and different from my jock world, though we do have some jocks.

Books are my escape *into* reality. In case you haven't figured it out, my life is like some dark fantasy. It's impossible to predict. I take my friends through the losers bracket when they *beg* me not to, just so I can have an extra shot at spending time with people who likely won't show anyway, and if they do, we'll squabble. I lie to people who have gone *far* out of their way to take care of me because the truth of my motives seems crazy and I'd be embarrassed telling it. Half the time I lie to *myself* because it's . . . it's just *easier*. I'm too smart for my own good, I guess, because I know all that—and have the vocabulary to describe it—and it causes huge arguments *inside* me, which probably means I shouldn't read so many books. How's *that* for circular thinking?

But I'm not about to stop reading books.

It's funny how I got in here. I saw the sign over by the teen section about three years ago, walked over to the desk, and said, "So how do I get into this book club?"

Sharon the Liberrian, as we call her, looked me up and down and said, "Show up."

Let me tell you about Sharon. This chick is *hot*—flaming red hair, close cropped on the sides and styled on top, a couple of really cool piercings, and you can see the edges of tats next to the top button on her blouse. And her face is, like, gorgeous.

"That's it?"

"That's it." She moved around the desk, put a hand in the middle of my back, and guided me toward a neon sign reading "Tattered Pages," where she ordered a cup of black coffee for herself and a hazelnut latte for me. "It's not a very big group, but every member is a lover of the tome, as I like to say. And it's not just a reader's club. We also write."

"Works for me."

"Good. Tell me about yourself."

"Do I have to?"

She laughed. "No. I can figure it out."

"How are you gonna do that?" I don't know why I was feeling confrontational; that part of me rises up on its own, whenever.

"By the books you like," she said. "And the books you don't."

Of course.

"One rule," she said. "What's said in book club, stays in book club. Cool?"

"Like, no rats. That's all?"

"Unless there's anything *you* want to know."

"How old are you?"

"I'm thirty-five."

"Are there boys?"

"In the club? Of course."

"How do you know they're not in there just because . . . you know, how you look."

"I couldn't care less why they're there, as long as they read, write, and participate."

"But . . ."

Her lips pursed and she leaned forward. "I'm married with two kids, young lady—kids I would murder Jesus for—

with a husband who plays in a band and rocks my world and is twice as hot as any guy you'll meet before you're twenty-five. What kind of question was that?"

"I was kind of messing with you."

"Well, you need to get better at it if you want to mess with *me*." She got up and walked behind the counter for a refill. "So you like books."

"I do. A lot."

"What do you like about them?"

"I don't know . . . you know . . . they tell the truth. At least the characters do."

"Want to know what got me interested in being a librarian?" She didn't wait for an answer. "*The Color Purple*."

"You became a librarian because of a movie?"

She laughs. "It was a book first. One you might really like."

"What did you like about it?"

"Did you watch the movie?"

"On cable."

"Then you know the *general* story. I guess I read it at the right time. It didn't matter that Celie was an uneducated black girl living in the south in the nineteen-thirties with a life completely different from mine. It mattered that she stood up. She took off her mask and stood up." She frowned at me, like she was trying to decide something. Then, "I was a foster kid, and I grew up scared, trying to be good just so I could stay."

"You were a foster kid?"

She nodded. "So are you, I'll bet," but again, didn't wait for an answer. "I felt so good after reading that book, I wanted to stand up, too, and write stories just like it. Trouble was, I couldn't write for shit, if you'll pardon the expression, so the next best thing was to find more books like it, read them, and hand them out."

"How'd you know I'm a foster kid?"

"Same way *you* recognize other kids like you."

So I've been part of our group for three years, and when I think of all the things I have going for me, it would be one of the last I'd be willing to give up. It's like, the world you have is the world you have, but books are the secret tunnel to the world you want.

Today Sharon asks us to introduce ourselves, because we have a new member, a tall, sandy-haired kid who doesn't seem to blink, but he also doesn't look right *at* anybody.

"Folks," she says, "this is Seth. Seth assures me he is a voracious reader who will be instantly willing and capable to add to our discussions. Did I get that right, Seth?"

"Most certainly," Seth says. His voice kind of *booms*.

We start clockwise around the circle giving just our names and the titles of one or two of our favorite books. Sharon knows anyone who stays any amount of time will come to their own conclusions about each of us and doesn't like to waste time on what kind of car or animal we'd be.

Judging from his shifting glances Seth *will* remember Maddy for her outstanding cleavage and the fact that she's sitting next to him and smells really good.

Sharon says, "Who wants to bring Seth up-to-date?"

Layton says, "I'll do it."

Maddy says, "Speak up, Lay. Make your voice like your pecs."

Blood rushes into Layton's face like he was flipped on his head. Maddy messes with him all the time. If he does make his voice like his pecs, it will be loud and clear. Layton is a *dedicated* non-steroid body-builder who's almost as shy as he is *built*, and though he never comes in show-offy tank tops, almost any T-shirt fits him like a coat of paint. "We're discovering *heroes*," he says. "For a while it looked like we'd never actually start reading another book because no one could agree on what that was, but then Sharon said we were all right—as in *correct*—and gave us a list of a hundred books to find them in."

"Which were just suggestions," Maddy says. "We can choose from that list or any book in any bookstore that can get us enough copies."

"So," Seth says, "*any* book."

Sharon nods. "Fiction, nonfiction, biography, science, history, you choose. We've fallen headlong into print looking for heroes." She hands Seth a sheet of her hundred picks. "The idea being, if we define them in print we might also find them in real life."

"And decide if we have any personal characteristics that could define *us* as heroes," Layton says.

Seth glances quickly at the list and sets it aside. "I think you will all ascertain in very short order that I am not a hero."

"We'll see," Sharon says, then looks to the rest of us. "If I remember correctly, and I always do, the final statement last week was, 'There are no heroes. Only heroic acts.' Did I get that right, Oscar?"

Oscar says, in his captivating accent, "Word for brilliant word."

"Go."

Oscar nods. "Like I said last time, choose any hero you wish, give me a little time, and I'll find something in his or her history that is definitely *not* heroic." Oscar came here from Cape Town, South Africa, several years ago, and always brings a different slant on any conversation. He was born "in the middle" of a black South African mother and a Dutch father, which, if you live in South Africa, creates an interesting life for you.

Mark says, "What about Jesus?" Very little of what we discuss doesn't go back through Nazareth for Mark.

"Dude," Oscar says, "I'm talking about somebody real."

"Nobody more real than Jesus," Mark says. Mark's what you might call an enigma—dresses head to foot in camo— head to knees in the summer—and holds *tight* to his Christian beliefs, though he never pushes them on you like some people. He also *acts* on them.

"*Pinocchio* is more real than Jesus," Oscar says back. "But let's remove Jesus and Muhammed and Buddha and Yoda and Obi-Wan Kenobi from the equation for now. If you consider so-called heroes we can trace, whether they're famous like Martin Luther King, Junior, or Nelson Mandela or Michael Jordan or the American Sniper guy or simply some lady who leaped in front of a car to snatch a rolling baby buggy from its path, they all may have performed heroic *acts*, but that's it. We create heroes because we don't like what human beings are really like."

Mark says, "Man, you are a hard-ass in the truest sense." He says it with humor and a certain admiration.

"That's because it's dangerous to have heroes," Oscar says.

Sharon says, "Because . . . "

"Because they aren't the truth. They get you thinking there's something wrong with you because if you're honest, you know you can never be like them."

Sharon nods. "Anyone else?"

Leah, my good friend, Hoopfest mate, and crazy-fast black chick (her term) from the A swim team, who joined about the same time I did, says, "I gotta go with Oscar. Last summer I'm lifeguarding at Witter pool and just as we're switching guard stations, two kids come running up from the river hollering that somebody's drowning. It's wicked hot and I've been listening to kids behind me jumping off the Mission Street bridge all afternoon. Anyway, I run across the park lawn, get over the fence and down to the edge where I see a kid trying to help another kid about fifteen yards from shore, but he's just making it worse. So I swim out, push the helper kid away, and pull the other one out. Head of the park department hears about it, calls the newspaper and a couple of TV stations, and next thing I'm a hero."

"Well, shoot," Mark says, "you were."

Leah scoffs. "That was easier for me than you carrying a sack of groceries across the street for an old lady, which is nice but not heroic. The TV and newspaper reporters were bending over backward to make me look like a way better person than I am. And braver. That kid couldn't have pulled me underwater with a rope tied to a sack of barbells. And I *sure* wasn't about to tell the reporters some of the shit I've done while they were busting their asses to make this a story about how not all teenagers threaten humanity." She laughs. "Especially African-American teenagers.

Sharon says, "So what are you saying?"

"I'm saying it wasn't even a heroic *act* and they made me a hero. People want things black or white—no pun—so that's how they wrap them."

"My point," Oscar says, "only things black and white are zebras and American referees."

Layton says, "American referees *are* zebras. We call 'em that."

"Zebras are striped horses," Oscar says. "Remember where I'm from."

Sharon closes her eyes. "Focus, people."

"I've been in church every Sunday and Wednesday night since, like, before I can remember," Mark says. "That's where *all* my heroes come from, starting with Jesus." He nods toward Oscar. "Sorry man, I just couldn't leave Him in with Yoda and Obi-Wan."

"The *hero* Jesus," Leah says.

Mark's eyebrows go up. "I guess. That WWJD thing . . . In my church you actually ask yourself that. And isn't that what a hero is—somebody you would follow?"

Leah laughs. "You'd get a better answer if you asked what *I* would do."

"I can end this foolishness." All eyes on Seth. His hand is raised, and he sits erect as a soldier. This kid would be out of place among out-of-place kids.

I say, "That would be deeply appreciated."

"I detect a note of sarcasm in your voice which I choose to ignore because I could be mistaken this early in our relationship," he says. "I should warn you I lack social skills. At least that's what I'm told, so if I offend you, don't be offended."

I say, "If you knew my family, you'd know social skills are lost on me."

"Be that as it may," he says, turning his head to include the rest of the group, "while many of you seem to have buried yourselves in make-believe—my favored terminology for fictitious tales—I have long been on a quest for real information, much of which I've found among the brain scientists."

Oscar whispers, "Uh-oh."

"Cynical facial expressions do not faze me, Oscar. As I

was saying . . . it would seem that the reason for the confusion experienced within your group—*our* group now that you've included me—likely comes from immaturity, and before you take issue, I mean that in the scientific sense."

Sharon says, "We don't take issue. Go on."

"The part of your brains that could logically put this all together," Seth says, "is simply not developed yet. Nor should it be. If my calculations are correct, the average age in this room, absent, of course, that of our leader," and he nods toward Sharon, "is about sixteen years, if my eyeballing of your ages were to prove accurate. Had I your birthdates I'd be more precise. At any rate, the frontal lobe, the *rational* portion of the brain, generally reaches full development around age twenty-three or twenty-four. Approximate numbers, but that means your brains are seven to eight years from making sense of some very obvious truths, so it's easy for you to create your heroes from emotion." He turns his palms up.

Leah says. "What about your brain, Seth?"

"There are a number of studies focused on brains like mine, and though the jury is still out, they may be quite advanced." He smiles slightly. "Of course there's no *real* jury."

"So while your brain is awaiting a verdict," Maddy says, "the jury is in on ours. What's the verdict?"

"Stupidity, pretty much," Seth says.

I laugh. "And you say you don't have social skills."

Seth ignores me. "It's not your fault, really, and it will get better. But until then, you are pretty much relegated to relying on *wishes* to take the lead in your decision-making. That's why the confusion. What *is* right only *seems* like *maybe* it is, but what you *want* to be right seems like it *really* is. That's why you're obsessed with this hero thing, and why you can't agree on it. Understand?"

"Thank you, Seth," Sharon says.

"Don't thank me; I'm merely the messenger. Thank the neuroscientists, whose books are out there for all of you to read. When you get tired of make-believe, that is."

"Apart from the unusual delivery," Sharon says as she backs Seth off with a look, ". . . thoughts?"

The unusual delivery doesn't bother me a bit. I come from roots where almost *any* delivery doesn't get delivered. "Is he right?"

"About what?" Sharon says.

"That we make things up to fit what we want them to be because we're . . . stupid?"

Mark sits forward, seemingly disturbed. "That's not exactly what he said. My takeaway is that we believe what we're told until there's reason not to, and the reasoning comes later. So, like, we *buy into* heroes someone else is selling."

Oscar shrugs, "Which makes my case. No heroes, just heroic acts. That must be disturbing to you, Mark."

Mark is pulling on the back of his hair. "C'mon man. Even if I let you put Jesus in the Yoda box, there's Gandhi? Einstein? Eisenhower? Abraham Lincoln?"

Leah says, "Serena Williams? Amelia Earhart? Jerrie Mock? Marilyn vos Savant?" She nods toward Mark. "Just balancing out the testosterone there, Camo Boy."

"Pray tell," says Oscar. "Who are Jerrie Mock and Marilyn vos Savant?

"Jerrie Mock," Leah says, "is the first woman to fly solo around the world, and Marilyn vos Savant has the highest-recorded IQ, like, *ever.*"

Oscar says. "We're slipping from hero to famous, and still, my theory holds. Gandhi was a racist, and Eisenhower cheated on his wife. Don't even know where to start on Lincoln. My lord, do I know more about your own folklore than you? Look, if you *have* to have heroes, simply choose anyone who's done more good than harm."

Seth's hand shoots up again. "Allow me to complicate things further. Imagine if you will, it's the summer of eighteen ninety-four in Leonding, Austria. You're twenty-five years old—therefore your frontal lobe is completely developed—and you're walking past a house fully engaged in flames. You hear the cries of a five-year-old boy coming from inside; you pull your shirt up over your face, rush in, and drag him out at great risk to life and limb. Are you a hero?"

"*Hell* yeah," Mark says. "They should have a parade for me."

I'm thinking: *1894, Leonding, Austria? That's pretty specific.*

"And well they might," Seth says. "You just saved a very young Adolf Hitler from the agony of going up in flames."

Mark deflates. "Very funny. Besides, that question was hypothetical."

"Smart people answer hypothetical questions with great frequency," Seth says. "It's an indicator of imagination, which Albert Einstein, whom you just cited as a hero, deemed quite essential to intelligence. Now add this to the mix, since you've proven yourself intelligent in the eyes of Albert Einstein. Imagine witnesses to this inferno begging you to save the boy, but you're magically blessed with foresight and therefore know how Baby Adolf will turn out. Would you let the future dictator roast and save the lives of six million Jews along with countless other various and sundry world citizens, at the risk of those witnesses forever damning you as a coward, or would you dash in and pull him out so you could have your parade?"

The trace of a smile crosses Mark's face. "Man, who are you?"

"I'll assume that question is rhetorical," Seth says. "Mine, on the other hand, is not. Have you an answer?"

Mark doesn't have an answer, neither does anyone else. You're either letting a child roast or killing six million Jews.

But Seth is on a roll. "Allow me to bring it closer to *your* sphere of influence," he says, and Mark breathes in. You don't want to judge Mark from appearance. All that camo stuff reminds me of Duck Dynasty dildos and elephant killers and other people who think if God didn't want us to shoot things he wouldn't have given us a trigger finger. But Mark must just like green and brown, because he always listens. "Bring it, Seth."

"My pleasure," Seth says. "Take the Nikos Kazantzakis book, *The Last Temptation of Christ*."

"I haven't read it," Mark says.

"I'm not surprised."

Sharon glances at her watch. "Short version, Seth."

Seth nods. "I won't go into the temptation itself, just the dilemma. Jesus needs to be betrayed to push the crucifixion/ resurrection thing into action. Only one guy in His entourage is up to it. Judas. Toughest of the bunch and loves Him most fiercely. If he agrees, Judas will be the scourge of all Christianity for all time. If he doesn't, the whole savior thing grinds to a halt. Judas says 'You're asking too much.' Jesus says, 'I know it's a lot.' Judas says, 'Master, could you do it?' Jesus says, 'No, you're the stronger one, Judas.' So basically, you have the hero to billions over two thousand plus years, saying to the villain to billions over that very same span, that *he's* the bigger hero. Hence Judas does what looks like a really bad thing but is actually a really good thing, if you happen to be a Christian and require a dead savior, that is." With a satisfied nod, Seth folds his arms. "Good and bad being relative, of course."

Oscar says, "So see? According to our resident alien, not only are there no heroes, but even heroic acts are suspect."

I'm heading back to the Howard's and almost get hit twice because my body's on my bike, but my head's floating somewhere in the stratosphere with Judas and Adolph Hitler. Traffic hazards aside, what I love about the book club is that you always walk away with something in your brain that's never been there before, and it's the only place in my life where I trust that people mean what they say, except for my therapist, of course. *And,* I mean, this Seth guy is a trip.

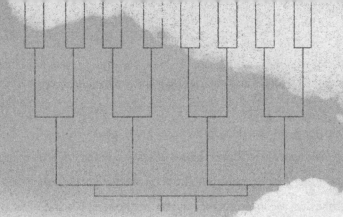

CHAPTER
SEVEN

"Wanna go shopping?"

Nancy made a whole meet. All by herself. No Walter sweet-talking me, no showing up after the last race, no "That was really great but I gotta go."

"Shopping would be cool." I notice her loose neck-to-ground clothing in this heat, devoid of ventilation. She's not dressed for shopping. She's dressed for shop *lifting.* "But Nancy, last time . . . "

"Don't be silly," she says. "Last time I was dirt poor. I got us what we needed. Walter is working two jobs. We have money now." She holds up her wallet, which hangs on a piece of twine around her neck. "This is legit. We'll buy some things. I haven't bought anything for my baby in forever."

It's Nancy and she's doing her best; if she gets caught, I'll disappear out a side door.

When Nancy "shops" alone, at any store that ends in –*mart*, she waits outside until just the right family comes along; then strikes up a conversation with one of them, appearing to be a member instead of a rotten robber. She grabs a cart and follows them down an aisle or two before peeling off and loading up.

When I'm with her, she introduces me to one of the greeters as we pass by, which she thinks makes her seem more normal and friendly, and makes them less likely to alert store detectives. Back in the days when I was in on it, we agreed that if she were caught, I would be horrified and she would weep with apology and hand everything back. I would run out of the store in tears screaming how I hated her, and the store detective would feel sorry for her and we'd get away with whatever she had stashed under *my* clothes. These days she's on her own.

It's been a risky profession, but she's never spent a night in jail, for *that* at least, so I guess you could say her skill set fits this particular chosen vocation.

She says, "Pick out a couple of tops you like."

I don't say I'm a girl who gets "tops I like" at Nordstrom's, but I can snag a couple of tank tops to work out in and no one will even notice, so I say okay and head to sportswear.

When I catch back up with Nancy, she's standing outside a dressing room fighting with a store employee over whether or not the skirt she just tried on was ripped before she went in there. All evidence says truth lies with the employee, but my money is on Nancy. She'll cry and threaten and debate and intimidate until this minimum wage indentured servant figures a way to give it to her at the drastically reduced price she was willing to pay in the first place.

Which is exactly what happens.

In the parking lot she transfers some items from a hiding spot any store clerk would *really* have to be dedicated to find, into the oversized bag that holds the torn skirt.

I never get a good answer, but I have to ask yet one more time. "Nancy, why do you do this shit? You said you had money."

She looks truly consternated. "I don't know, baby. I do have money . . . it's just . . . it's so easy. It seems like such a *waste*."

"If they catch you, you could go to jail."

She stuffs the bag into the back of her ratty car. "Hasn't happened yet."

"Chances increase every time," I say.

"So I spend a couple of days in the hoosegow," she says, nodding toward the backseat. "Whaddaya think all that is worth? I mean really worth. What I paid for those blouses of yours would cover the cost of the material and whatever they pay those poor China ladies or Vietnams. You think the people what own that store wear this shit? I'm just evenin' up . . . puttin' a little balance back in the world."

Like I said, no good answer. I guess if I'd lived with the Howards full-time from birth this wouldn't seem so normal, but it is what it is, as they say.

"Let's get a coffee."

She glances at her wallet.

"You can buy with your savings. There's a Starbucks a block over."

"They don't like me too much there," she says.

"Why not?"

"Look at me, Annie," she says, holding her arms out crucifixion style. "Nobody wants me in their place."

Sometimes she worries about her appearance—and maybe her hygiene—and sometimes she couldn't care less. She's a full-sized lady, as they say, but no bigger than a lot of people since she's been with Walter, but this must be one of those days. It might help if she were a little pickier about the clothes she steals. "Tough," I say. "We're going to Starbucks. It's on me."

The Starbucks employees don't even blink when we come in. That's just how Nancy feels when she goes anywhere. There are times I want to skin her alive; she makes promises I know *way* better than to believe, and she whines and snarls and judges her way through life. But if you could see the look on her face when we walk through the door, the trepidation that says, "Please don't look at me and if you do, please don't turn away," well, you'd buy Nancy a coffee, too.

"You got a boyfriend yet?"

"Nope. No boyfriend."

"Baby, you're a catch. What are you waitin' for?"

"Nancy, I'm seventeen. I have plenty of time to get a boyfriend." What I don't say is if I *did* have a boyfriend, I wouldn't tell her because she'd be telling me how to keep him, and *that* conversation is gross.

"I had my way with the best-lookin' boy in my class when I was *fifteen,*" she says.

"Nancy, that can't be. You dropped out after sixth grade. You'd have been twelve."

"You always think you're so smart. I was fifteen when I got out of sixth."

Jeez. "That would have made *him* twelve."

"Okay," she says. "I get my times mixed up. But . . . Annie, I don't want you to be alone, is all. It hurts so much. . . . "

I know most seventeen-year-olds have already gone through their first half-dozen boyfriends, and there were a couple of guys I was pretty excited about in eighth grade, but neither of them made it into high school, and I've read enough to know if you grew up like I did, there's a pretty good chance your mate selection skills might be, like, primitive.

"Speaking of boyfriends, who's this guy Sheila was with?"

"Sheila don't tell me nothin'. Hell, I thought she was with that dyke."

"Yvonne is her friend, Nancy. This was some guy named Butch."

"Never heard of no Butch," she says. "Why?"

I'm hesitant to tell, but . . . "He knocked Sheila around pretty good, and I found some marks on Frankie."

"You tell CPS?"

"I was gonna call my old caseworker, but Frankie would end up someplace completely unfamiliar, and nobody's going to keep him for long. He's back at our place now, but the Howards' license is specialized just for me."

"They could lose it," she says. "Foster parents are mandatory reporters." One place Nancy *is* an expert is the workings of children's services. "He could come with me."

"C'mon, Nancy. *I* can't come with you, and I'm your kid."

"Let's talk about something else. I wanted this day to be about you and me. What about Thanksgiving this year? You going to make it, or you gonna follow Foster Pop's rules?"

"I haven't missed one yet, and I've been grounded every time I was caught."

Nancy holds a gala "family" Thanksgiving dinner every year at Quik Mart. Yeah, the convenience store; and it's way more bizarre than it sounds. I've had to sneak to it every year, because if you think Pop balks at my connecting up at my public sports events, well. . . . Marvin thinks it's the coolest thing ever, which gives an indication of just how strange things get.

"It's in November, Nancy. Why are you asking me now?"

"It was all I could think of to change the subject," she says, and stands to get another sugar. "I think you should keep up this swimming thing, by the way. It looks like a lot of fun."

"If it looks like so much fun, they have Masters' swimming."

She looks down, appraises. "You think I'm putting *this* body in a swimming suit?"

"If you did it every day, that body would look really different," I tell her.

"I s'pose," she says, and stares out the window.

It's times like this that I just wish I could take *care* of my mother. I remember her screaming out the stories of her own childhood in times when she was tired of my whining—how she had to hide from her uncle and a couple of her cousins, how her father used to swing her around by the hair to show his friends how tough she was. I mean he lifted her off the ground and swung her around and around like a sack of

85}

potatoes. And if she cried or yelled, he dropped her. When I think of that, my throat closes over with hopelessness.

I feel guilty.

"You busy?" Pop stands in the doorway to my room where I'm stretched out on the bed reading the back cover of *Bastard out of Carolina*, a book Maddy said I'd hate, but would relate to.

I say, "Not really,"

"Time to talk?"

"Sure."

He sits at the foot of the bed, takes a deep breath. Uh-oh. "Momma and I have been talking about . . . your family."

"The Boots."

"The ones and onlys."

"What about them?"

"We've been pretty lax about contact. I know, you see them in public—at games and swim meets. I think it's more frequent than that."

I freeze inside, but hold his gaze.

"Well?"

"I run into them sometimes. Mostly Nancy. You know, she's all over the place."

"I think it's more intentional than that."

I shrug and look away.

"That's what I thought. It needs to stop, Annie."

I hesitate. "Or what?"

"I haven't wanted to go there," he says, "and I'd appreciate it if you didn't force me to."

"Pop, it doesn't even affect me anymore. I know when I was little and they'd send me home, I'd come back a little shit, but I'll bet you can't even tell when I've seen them now."

"Remember back at Hoopfest when you bludgeoned that girl on the court because Nancy didn't show? Remember all the times you've come back from an event and gone straight to your room, wouldn't say hello or sit with us? After all we've done?"

"I go to my room because I don't want to have *this* very conversation."

"Annie, I've told you, I won't be lied to."

Then don't ask me questions. That one stays in my head.

"I know you went to Sheila's."

Dang! "How did you know that?"

"It doesn't matter how I know. It matters that I know."

"We ordered pizza."

"Mmm-hmm. How did that end?"

I surrender. "The pizza ended on the floor. But I wasn't the one to come uncorked."

Pop stands, palms the back of his neck—a warning sign.

"I don't want this to turn into one of our epic struggles, but you're going to be a senior in high school. You can't go out into the world lying to people."

"Actually, people do it all the time."

I'm lucky this time. Pop really doesn't want to get into this all the way, and he's learned that threatening me is about the best way to assure I'll do what I'm not supposed to.

Back in the day, when Nancy screwed up yet one more time and I got sent back, I was a handful. I hoarded food, disappeared things that were really important to Momma and Pop, threw temper tantrums that scared even *me*. They responded with "time out," which was basically "go to your room," then started taking things away when I didn't straighten up—my iPod, books, games, whatever, until the only things in my room were my bed, my dresser, and me. When I was like that, they just couldn't cost me enough. They won all the battles, but I won the war, because what they didn't understand was, they could throw me out into a snowbank and nothing would have changed. My insides were so crazy mixed up that all I could count on was my own stubbornness.

"I don't like those struggles, either, Pop," I say now.

He takes a deep breath and stares out my window. He really should send Momma on these missions. Or better, Marvin.

"I'm going to leave it at that," he says, "because I promised Jane I wouldn't lay down an ultimatum unless I have to." He pats me on the knee and walks out.

Pop has a way of laying down an ultimatum without laying down an ultimatum. I get it; if I keep hooking up with my family, I could be on my way out. That's the only card he has left to play.

"If you wanna keep favored child status," Marvin says, "you have to take the good with the bad."

Marvin had waited five minutes after Pop left before coming in to commiserate.

"What's the good?"

"Serious? iPhone, car, allowance, dictator dad too busy to follow up on his 'dictates' most times . . . "

"How did he know about me going to Sheila's place?"

"Who knows? He's caught me sometimes when I thought there was *no* way. I suspect he may have spies."

"What?"

"Who knows? He talks to you more than me." He considers that a second. "Thank God."

"He talks *at* me."

"You know the other thing he's worried about with you, don't you?"

"*Which* other thing?"

"That you're kick-ass," he says. "You know, violent."

"I'm not *violent*."

Marvin smiles. "A little aggressive, maybe, but yeah, no bodies lie dormant in your wake."

"Marvin, 'bodies lying dormant in my wake' would be *dead*. Can't you just say *dead*? And where did you get that he thinks I'm violent?"

"Same place I get all my information . . . through the heat grate in my bedroom. Fancy house like this one shouldn't have built-in walkie-talkie, but it does. If you lay your ear right next to it, you can hear Mom and Dad talking in bed." His face reddens. "Unfortunately, that's not all you hear."

"You listen to your parents . . . "

"Collateral damage," he says. "I only listen when I think my hide is on the line. For a small fee, I'll work in your behalf."

"How'd you get so smart?"

"Ginkgo biloba," he says. "Hey, everyone thinks guys my age are stumbling into puberty trying to figure out what to do with our di . . . private parts. I know exactly what to do with my private parts; I just don't know who to do it with." He smiles wider. "Except for, you know, myself."

"*Way* too much information."

He laughs. "Remember the kitten?"

"The one you had for a week? Yeah, what does that have to do with anything?"

"Remember how Dad said he got it for me so I'd learn responsibility?"

"Uh-huh."

"That's not why he got it." He deepens his voice, imitating Pop. "Marvin, it's time you learned to get serious. It is incumbent on you to take care of this little fella. Your room will be his home. His very existence depends on you. Welcome to my world."

"But he was here a week. He ran away, right?"

"Yeah," Marvin says. "In a basket on the back of my bike to Jenny Peterson's house."

"Why? He was darling."

"Do you know what a kitten does when he sees something moving under the covers?" He doesn't wait for an answer. "He pounces!"

OMG! "Pop gave you that kitten to . . . "

" . . . keep me from, how should I put this . . . *practicing*. I say, "That's just cruel."

"I'd wake up in the morning . . . "

"I don't need to hear this."

" . . . rise to lock the door . . . "

"Did I say I don't need to hear this?"

" . . . one move, and *whack!*" Marvin smiles with the satisfaction of having told a story he thinks is funny while grossing me out.

That's Pop's grotesque idea of a sense of humor.

"Anyway that's not *all* I think about," Marvin says. "I think a *lot* about how to outfox my dad, but mostly that leads to dreams of bulking up in the gym to get his hopes up, then turn out for high school drama. Unfortunately, us drama dudes are memorizing soliloquies when we could be doing push-ups."

"They aren't mutually exclusive, you know . . . drama and push-ups."

Marvin makes a muscle, only the muscle doesn't make. "Yeah, I know, I know."

"Listen," I say. "If you hear through the heat grate that my eviction is imminent, you'll let me know, right?"

"'Course I will. But you gotta know, you've got *the* very best firewall."

"Really. What's that?"

"Mom."

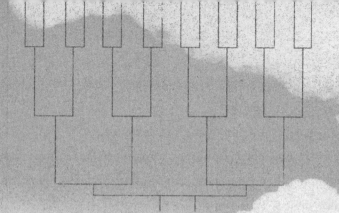

CHAPTER
EIGHT

Two days after the non-ultimatum ultimatum from Pop, Leah offers me a ride home from book club, so I throw my bike into the back of her pickup and hop in shotgun.

As we're pulling up to the house, she says, "Hey, listen, I was over at you guys' practice the other day watching my little sister."

"You won't be able to watch her there for long," I say. "She gets faster by the day."

"Yeah," Leah says, "if we were closer in age, she'd be giving me a run, but, that's not my point. Uh, I don't know how to say this. . . . "

"You saw me swim."

Her long, graceful fingers tap the steering wheel. "That's a generous depiction."

I laugh. "A better one is 'not drowning.'"

"Uh-huh. 'Not drowning' is easier on land. Annie, you might look good in a Speedo, but trust me, you're a sunbather. Your shine is on the court."

"I like to try stuff."

She glances sideways at me. "I could give you a list of things to try that would give you a longer life-span, but if you're going to do this, why don't you let me work with you . . . you know, on your stroke."

"You'd do that? Isn't that, like, the very definition of *quixotic*?"

"Call it community service. Run in and get your suit and we'll shoot over to the pool. I've got about an hour and a half before I meet Tim."

"That would be *so* cool, but right now I gotta get in the house and see if Frankie has cut Marvin into small pieces and hidden them like Easter eggs. Could we do it later? Like maybe tomorrow?"

We make a date and Leah waits for me to haul my bike out of the pickup bed, then speeds off.

Standing in the hall entryway, I hear voices, tiptoe to the partially open door of the converted playroom Momma has set up for Frankie, and squat against the wall.

Marvin has squeezed into the tiny rocking chair with his back to me while Frankie lies on his stomach holding a conversation between a plastic bear and a small teddy bear—toys from the stash Momma keeps for those unexpected visits. He uses a high voice for the plastic bear, lower for the teddy.

Plastic Bear: We don't need no dads.

Teddy Bear: How come?

Plastic Bear: 'Cause they do drugs and go to jail. An' they hurted our mom.

Teddy Bear: Moms do drugs, too.

Plastic Bear: But sometimes moms stop and buy you stuff. And sometimes they take you away from dads. Dads are bad. They go to jail. My dad is in jail. My new dad didn't go to jail yet."

Teddy Bear: Is he goin', do you think?

Plastic Bear: Maybe, yeah, a lot of dads go to jail. My old dad wants to kill my mom, but he's five hundred miles away. My new dad might, too. I just need a mom, not a dad. They always go to jail.

I creep in and park behind Marvin. Frankie ignores me.

I whisper. "How long has this been going on?" Marvin glances at his iPhone. "Hour or so."

"You've been watching this for an *hour*?"

"It's like you can see his world. He calls any guy Sheila brings home 'Dad,' and I think she's brought some bad ones."

"Only kind she knows."

"Man," he whispers, "if you just watch, or join in when he wants you to, you learn some crazy stuff." He watches a minute longer. "This goes round and round. He wants his mom *bad,* but she won't protect him; she loves him when she's not on drugs and bails when she is."

Marvin looks up at me. "Why are you *crying*?"

"It's mostly about rhythm," Leah says. "Two kicks per stroke and you have to move *forward.* Think like a dolphin."

"Dolphins are supposed to be really smart, right?" I say.

"Even *dumb* dolphins swim," she says. "Get the *feel* of it."

"I *feel* better on land."

She laughs. "If I remember right, this was a *choice.* What did you do to get yourself in all the fly events? That's the stroke you learn last, if at all."

"That's the stroke that *gives* you a stroke," I say, "but there's less competition. Keeps me in the water."

Leah gives me a good half hour of detailed instruction: Get the timing, swim till the stroke starts to deteriorate, then stop; if I swim after my stroke falls apart, my body will learn it wrong.

"One thing you already know as an athlete," she says, "never do *anything* half-assed when you can do it full-assed."

Pop and I are at a standoff through the rest of my "swimming season," such as it is. His silence has amped up his irritation at me for not playing elite basketball; he simply won't accept that I won't get with the program and hop on the bus—and the plane—to go up against the top competition in the sport I'm best at.

"I don't want to burn out," I tell him.

"Which is why you'll *never* reach your potential," he says. "You kids. All you want is to have fun. Get a little bored with something and you're 'burned out,' off trying something else. The true elite players in any sport know *repetition*."

The only repetition I'm sure of is Pop saying the same thing over and over and over, but I keep that to myself. He'll have me doing push-ups until my arms melt if I challenge his expertise as a motivator.

"Do you know how Michael Jordan became Michael Jordan?" he asks.

"Because his parents named him that?"

"Because he *never* took his eye off his goal. Everything he played, he played all out. He'd fight and scratch every second of a meaningless one-on-one game, whether he was a point ahead or ten. When Michael got you down, he put his foot square on your neck." He takes a deep breath. "Annie, what you don't realize is, *now* is the time when you get hardwired for athletics. So many talented athletes think they can coast when the years are easy, when they're twice as talented as their peers. But with every level you move up, dozens more mediocre athletes fall away, and the competition becomes that much tougher. Kids who were fabulous athletes in high school walk into a university with a whole team of kids who were fabulous athletes in high school. The ones with fire in their belly make it. Is that so hard to understand?"

It isn't. *He* doesn't understand that I'm not Michael Jordan, or more specifically, Kelsey Plum. I have fire in my belly, but it's not burning to make me a top high school recruit for some university. I don't think that far ahead. On the court during the season, fire is *all* I've got. I never let my teammates or my coach down—if you don't count Hoopfest losers bracket, but that's different—and I can't start to tell you how I hate to embarrass myself. Way too often that fire is anger, I get that; Pop is right about my temper putting my game in jeopardy. Half the time I can't even put my finger on what I'm mad at. He and I wouldn't come to these loggerheads if he helped me understand what motivates me instead of deciding what *should* motivate me.

No matter. School will start in less than a month, which means volleyball and basketball in earnest, at which point all of the above will come into play. Pop gets highly supportive and highly critical, and I get highly motivated and highly manipulative. In book club, Seth said some things can only exist in a state of great tension. He was talking about science, but it's sure true about Pop and me.

So the end of summer is the end of my "frivolous" athletic endeavors for the year, but I swear I'm coming to enjoy being anonymous in my sport. Leah's work on my stroke has given me a whole different feel for my body in the water, and even though I'm no Dara Torres—a name I wouldn't even know to drop if it weren't for Leah—I am no longer disqualifying myself by walking the last five yards and have actually picked up some points for our team. I've also dazzled Janine—the architect of my butterfly torture—with my tenacity and my improvement.

And there's something about the way this butterfly stroke *feels* when done right. It requires a kind of physical *congruence* that almost works on its own. What's really cool is, for the last meet of the season I'm going to have supporters who 1) I really want to impress and 2) will actually show up. See, once Leah started working with me, she recommended *Swimming to Antarctica* as a book club read.

It wasn't an easy sell.

"The woman who wrote this book is *tough*," Leah said when she introduced it. "This is some seriously grueling shit. Forget Diana Nyad, this Lynne Cox chick swam the Bering Strait. She actually swam over a mile in Antarctica. In a Speedo!"

"And why, pray tell," Oscar said, "would we read a book with seriously grueling shit?"

"Because we're going full *female aqua*," Leah said, "to celebrate Annie on the front end of her swimming career, me in the middle, and Lynne Cox when she was at her apex, got it?" She withdrew a full-sized Swiss Army knife from her purse, pulled out the corkscrew, narrowed her eyes, and said, "And because I know your ride."

I said, "Uh, Leah, I'm with Lynne Cox. This is my swimming apex, believe me."

Seth's arm flew up. "Ms. Sharon, do we or do we not have a rule about weapons?"

"Actually, Seth," Sharon said, "that's not *exactly* a weapon. . . . " She looked sideways at Leah. "Right, Leah?"

Leah smiled. "I was using it as punctuation."

Seth said, "So Oscar doesn't really have to worry about you setting free the stuffing in his upholstery? Or creating an unsightly scratch the length of his car?"

Leah held up the knife. "Maybe you can help me out, Seth. I want him to *worry* about those things, but I'm not going to *act* on either. What should I do?"

Seth's head shook no like a small tightly wound bobblehead. "You've blown it by stating your intent." He took a deep breath and almost established eye contact with her. "I was led to believe you were one of our more intelligent members."

"Even geniuses slip up."

"True," Seth said, "but you have to admit, showing your hand that way was a pretty basic slipup. Crass, even."

Leah nodded. "I think I can save this," she said. "Oscar has been known, on semi-frequent occasion, to ingest substances that alter his perception. What do you think would happen if I wait a week or so and recommend the book as if for the first time, in hopes he doesn't even remember it happened?"

Seth frowned, glanced at Oscar, who smiled and shrugged. "I suppose there's a possibility. We've certainly heard him repeat himself often enough. However, I'd be surprised if your chances are fifty-fifty."

"In which case, I just won't mess up his car," Leah said. "In fact we can avoid all of this, and all other threats, by giving me a big yes vote on this book."

It was unanimous. We're reading *Swimming to Antarctica*.

Flash forward two weeks to the last meet of the season; I'm on the deck with the rest of my teammates who I probably wouldn't recognize on the street, out of their Speedos, but I'm moving around encouraging everyone because my book club friends have read the book and filled the bleachers, and are chanting our name—the Anchors—while Coach Rick goes over who'll be swimming which events and calling out personal bests from memory. He says, "Remember, it's good to take down the competition, but it's even better to beat your old self."

Whispers into my ear, "Is that your entourage?"

I look over my shoulder at Janine. "Kind of. My book club."

"Who's the woman with them?"

"That would be Sharon the Liberrian; she's our unchallenged leader.

"This is the biggest crowd you guys have had all summer."

"And we will not disappoint," I say, nodding toward my anonymous teammates.

"Um-hmm," she says. "Well, it should be interesting." She starts to walk away.

I say, "Hey, Janine?"

"Yeah?"

"Thanks."

"For what?"

"For kicking my butt this summer," I say. "For keeping me swimming this god-awful butterfly until I got it."

She gives me the look that says we both know why.

"Listen," I say. "I was a bitch for messing with you."

She smiles. "Go be ruthless."

I live a compartmentalized life; that's what Mr. Novotny used to call it. He said it was a life skill, made necessary by the differences in my worlds. If I acted around my bio family the way I act with my friends, or vice versa, I'd have a lot of 'splainin' to do, as they say, but it works because there's so little chance of my worlds colliding.

Today my worlds collide.

The book club is in the bleachers chanting the names of as many of my teammates as they could collect, when something happens that *never* happens. Nearly the entire Boots clan troops across the park and onto the bleachers: Nancy, *Rance*—the Boo Radley of the Inland Northwest—the lovely Sheila trailed by Yvonne and Frankie.

I don't see firsthand what happens next because I'm hyperventilating on the blocks when it starts and in the water for the blastoff.

As I learn later, Sheila, who *must* be high, is convinced these people are actually here to *taunt* me, that no one could be here to root for the kind of swimmer I am, and they're calling us "Anchors" which *has* to be a rip, and what a bunch of nerds anyway. She relays that shiny nugget to Nancy, who walks up to *Seth* of all people and says, "Who you all here makin' fun of?" Seth only partially hears her because of the chanting and assumes she just wants the name of their champion. He says, "That would be the girl in the maroon racing suit," and Nancy says, "They're all in maroon racing suits, you idiot," and Seth points again and says, "Her name's Annie, and it's impolite to call me that. Judging from appearances, it's likely a more apt description of you."

Nancy asks Seth how he'd like a fist in his pimply face, to which Seth, who hears *no* question as rhetorical, says he wouldn't like that very much and why doesn't she pick on somebody her own enormous size. That brings quick escalation, and Sharon bails out of her seat to see if she can calm the waters *outside* the pool. Frankie begins running around the bleachers with his fingers in his ears shrieking like a referee's whistle, while Marvin hollers, "Mrs. Boots! Mrs. Boots! Everything's cool, we're rooting for Annie, just like you!" but Nancy has grabbed the Annie Boots enthusiast nearest her, which is Leah, by the shirt, ready to push her off the side of the bleachers which would be a really bad idea unless Leah lands on her head and is totally paralyzed because, well, if you want to injure Leah you better make sure Leah is *injured;* and if she is, you *really* better watch out for Tim.

For the first time I finish first in the fifty fly—all the girls who have gotten good have moved up to the B team—and I come up out of the water jubilant, turn to give my entourage a raised fist, only to see bedlam.

This is my fourth grade classroom experience on hallucinogenics. When something gets into Nancy's head, even the truth won't knock it out. She is certain her daughter has been publicly disparaged on a day when she not only made it on time, but brought the entire Boots crew, and somebody has to pay, and on this day if you're yelling your head off for the Anchors, it's you. To amp it up, this is the first day in the history of all Bootses everywhere that Sheila sides with Nancy.

I pull myself out of the water and race through the gate, hoping to stop this ahead of any arrests and before Leah hears the N-word, a staple in Sheila's verbal arsenal. I reach Nancy just as Leah is ready to punch her lights out—this wouldn't be happening if I had kept my two worlds completely apart—immobilize Nancy into a bear hug, and whirl her at the same moment Leah unleashes a roundhouse that catches me on the back of the head. Nancy and I tumble onto the grass, me landing on top which is very lucky for me. This could go on forever if Yvonne, who has kept herself completely out of the mayhem, doesn't scream, "WHERE'S FRANKIE?"

The Boots clan freezes, because they know who Frankie is, and the Annie Boots faithful freeze because the Boots do.

No Frankie.

In what has to be record time Sharon and Marvin, of all people, have everyone organized and we pour through the park calling Frankie's name.

To no response.

Mission Park is a sprawling city park. The pool sits adjacent to Mission Street, a busy two-way four-lane, with a playground to the south and family picnic grounds to the east. It's midweek so the place isn't packed, but Washington Water Power employees are eating lunch along with picnicking families, so *some*one had to see a five-year-old, screaming like a one-man merry-go-round off its hinges, going *poof*! But no one did. Suddenly we're all frantically searching the bushes and behind the outbuildings and the backseats of cars in the parking lot.

Sirens blast toward us while Sheila screams "No cops! No cops!" which ends her alliance with Nancy. Rance stands in the middle of it all like the ghost he is.

And Frankie is gone.

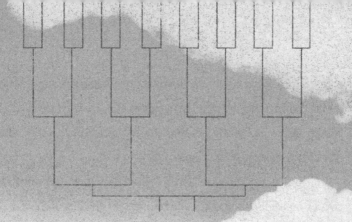

CHAPTER
NINE

He was there and then he wasn't. With as many people running around hurtling accusations and howling epithets, as much attention as was directed at us and as many smart phones as *had* to be there, it's almost impossible to imagine no one saw where he went.

But no one saw where he went.

Leah's first thought is the river. She sprints across the park and over an *eleven-foot chain-link* fence; jogs up and down the river's edge, but sees only calm waters. Thank God.

The responding cops and EMTs reorganize the search, block off the parking lot, and check all exiting cars.

Sheila has become less than no help, alternately screaming,

threatening, then breaking down in rapid circular succession while Yvonne tries to calm her by offering weed, which makes Nancy nervous, but this is Washington, and it's legal, maybe not smart, but legal.

I think I read, or saw on TV, that after the first hour or two of a child's disappearance, chances of finding him or her plummet. By four o'clock my sinking feeling has sunk. I called Momma first chance I got, and she called Pop, who shot over from work. There will be a long discussion about contact with the devil clan, and as much as I hate anticipating that, I'm worried that somehow this is my fault. It's crazy to want something so much that you forget who might get trampled if you get it.

The search at the park turned up nothing; Sheila has gone to the police station to file a report that I'm sure won't include her inattention, and as the sun lowers in the sky Leah and I are driving through neighborhoods adjacent to the park with Tim, who came running in response to Leah's text, at the wheel, on the off chance that Frankie got so rattled at the chaos that he just took off. I can barely breathe.

"They'll find him," Tim says. "A kid doesn't just vanish."

"Kids vanish all the time," I say. "Somewhere, I have a brother. I have no idea if he's even alive. His bio dad snatched him and left the state, then lost him to CPS. Kids disappear."

"C'mon, Annie," Leah says, "this is different."

"Yeah, well, tell you what's about to happen with my drug-crazed whore of a sister. She'll get on TV and cry and say what a wonderful little guy her Frankie was and how desperate and brokenhearted she is, and when it dies down she'll double her drug use and Frankie will just be another awful Boots memory."

"You're running *way* ahead. The cops have his picture and he'll be all over the news."

"There's no license number or car description. Unless someone actually spots Frankie, there are no clues."

Leah can be optimistic all she wants, but a kid gets grabbed from a public park for two possible reasons and they're both bad.

"I know what you're thinking," Leah says. I expect her to say *Don't think it.* "I'd be scared, too. I *am* scared."

I have a rule about crying, like maybe twice a year in really bad times, but I burst into tears. I mean, my eyes are *raining.* Leah pulls me to her. My losers bracket antics are supposed to cause groundings and family discord and chance meetings that turn out empty—the normal chaos of a Boots' kid's life. They are not supposed to end in a lost child.

When I'm emptied out, Leah says they'll take me

home and then keep looking, but I do *not* want to have the confrontation that is surely waiting there, and I don't need anyone saying the bad things I've already said about Sheila. I don't want to go on the attack the way I do when I'm scared or threatened, and I *sure* don't want to sit in front of the local news on TV, learning that nothing has been learned.

So we cruise the neighborhoods a couple more hours, then Tim drops Leah and me at Revel 77, a local late-night coffee place on the South Hill, where I text Momma because I know she'll back Pop off from demanding I come home so we can talk this to death. Pop always thinks he has to teach you the lesson you just learned.

I get a latte and Leah gets a coffee and sits on my side of the table where we stare out the window, happy that the tattooed barista doesn't know us from Adele and Beyoncé.

"I hate my family."

"And you love your family and you hate your family and you love your family," Leah says. She squeezes me, like, *tight*. "We don't pick 'em."

"Frankie's like me. If he had a brain he'd scream bloody murder until someone besides a kidnapper got him away from my sis. But two days at our place and he's aching to get back. I did exactly the same thing. Mr. Novotny told me they'd have pulled the plug before I hit kindergarten if I hadn't sabotaged every placement so I could get back to my clueless parents. I just wanted to give them one more chance to want me."

"You were a little kid," Leah says. "Kids go back to what's familiar, and besides, you know and I know Nancy's not all bad."

"Sometimes I know it and sometimes I don't."

"Well, when you don't, come ask me," Leah says. "You gotta give her points for *wishing*. She wishes she could be different, and I'll bet she tries really hard, at least in her own head."

"*Nothing* lasts with her, Leah. I mean, you're right; every promise she makes is heartfelt. But the shelf life of a Nancy Boots promise is, like, twelve hours."

"Well that's twelve hours more than a lot of kids get. I landed in the sweet part of my family, but I have relatives who've crapped on their families in ways even you wouldn't believe."

I know she's right. I don't have to spend much time in the library to read stories that make me feel lucky. Still . . .

She bumps me with her shoulder. "Family holds the strongest pull. It's brain science. Ask Seth. We get a nine-month head start with our mothers, no matter how messed up they are. Rhythms; heartbeats. We eat what they eat, share their fluids."

"Yeah," I say, "and whatever else they put in while we're there."

"There's that," she says. "Biology doesn't separate vitamins from drugs."

"All I know is, Nancy couldn't choose any of us over herself, and Sheila's the same way. How is Frankie not *chained* to her when they go out in public?"

"Not everyone should be allowed to have kids," Leah says.

"It was worse for Sheila than me." I hate to stop trashing her because it's the only thing that feels good, but right now I want Leah to understand, even though I've already told her this a thousand times. "I went back to the same placement every time; Momma and Pop always left the door open. Sheila blew out of *every* placement, and some of them were *way* worse than living with Nancy. But either way, they'd put her back when no way Nancy was ready, because there was just no other place. And now look at her. She's not even two years older than me and she seems fifty. And dumb—lets every new guy be Frankie's dad, drags him all over town, forgets he's with her if she's not tripping over him."

Leah says. "Maybe your fosters shouldn't have given her cover. They might have found him a good place by now, like they did for you."

"Maybe, but who keeps a kid with his, what do you call

them . . . maladaptive behaviors? I mean, how do you explain Frankie to some unsuspecting foster home?"

"C'mon, how hard could he be to handle?"

I remind her of some of his less ingratiating habits.

"I see what you mean."

"Hey, Annie. Thought I might find you here." We look up to see Walter. "This party private, or one or the other of you want to buy me a coffee?"

Leah stands, gives him a light bop on top of his head, and walks to the counter.

Walter picks up a napkin reaches over and wipes a tear from under my eye. "Rough day, huh?"

"You hear anything?"

"Heard your mom and sister screaming at each other," he says.

"That's always pleasant."

"They're supposed to be sitting by the phone waitin' for news, but it's your momma screaming at Sheila for not taking care of her kid, Sheila screamin' back at your momma for not taking care of *her*."

"My old social worker calls that 'shit rolling downhill.'"

"Guess social workers are good for *somethin'*."

I watch Leah coming with Walter's coffee through a nearly empty shop. "How did you know where we'd be?"

Leah sets the coffee in front of Walter, who picks it up and grins. "I keep an eye on you," he says. "I know you sneak off here when you want to be alone."

"You follow me?"

"Sometimes. Don't worry; it ain't creepy."

"When did *that* start?"

"Believe it or not, your mom likes to know you're okay. Be a little harder to track you, now that I told you."

"I'll make it easy. You have my permission."

"Listen," Walter says, "you saw the marks on Frankie's arm, right? When they were fresh?"

"Yeah."

"How bad?"

"Dark, swollen. Pretty big. Not as bad as Sheila's face."

"And you think it was this last boyfriend, Butch something. . . . "

"His name doesn't matter," I say. "They're all the same guy. Love and assault are the same to Sheila."

He sips his coffee, thanks Leah. "He best not let *me* catch up to him."

I ask, "What's going to happen, Walter?"

"I don't know. I went over to the police station to see if I could add any information; you know, told them I spend time with the kid's grandmother. They weren't all that interested. Don't guess I carry a lot of weight anywhere near the courthouse. They file me under 'vagrant.'"

Leah says, "Vagrant?"

"I'm an old biker," Walter says. "Only way my opinion could mean less is if I could be identified as black." He catches himself. "No offense."

Leah just shakes her head. "You ain't tellin' me nothin' new, Mr. Multicolored Biker. Even rich black chicks with four-point-oh grade averages who could save their kids from drowning get stopped by the cops more often than coincidence should allow." She glances at her phone. "Tim's on his way to pick us up—five minutes."

"Walter, do you think it would help if we went to the police and backed you?"

"Wouldn't hurt," he says. "This thing'll only be hot awhile. Best give them ever'thing we can. I was impressed they were right on top of it." He finishes his coffee and stands. "I'll leave you young ladies to your rat killin'. Got a bit of a hike home. Thanks for the coffee."

Leah stands with him. "We're done here, Walter. Tim will give you a ride."

"'Preciate it," Walter says, just as Tim pulls up outside.

We drop Walter at his place instead of at Nancy's because he needs a breather before connecting with Nancy again.

After you hear the ten ways Sheila has of calling Nancy a bitch once or twice, it just gets tedious.

Before he walks into his place, he puts his hands on my shoulders and says, "Don't you worry too much, Annie. Got a feelin' this'll turn out in the long run." It doesn't seem realistic, but I appreciate it.

I tell Leah and Tim I'd treat them to a movie or something, just because I don't want to go home, but Leah's heard enough from me about my struggles with Pop to know I'm stalling.

"That would be cool," she says, "but all you'd be doing is putting off a conversation with your foster dad that you're going to have sometime; plus Tim and I swim early."

"Way too early," Tim says.

"Look," Leah says, "when he starts in about your messed-up family, just tell him *later* and get to your room. I don't know about you, but my *room* is the safest place on the planet, and I'm not at war with anyone."

Pop asks where I've been before I can even close the front door.

I say, "With Leah and Tim."

His eyes narrow. "It would have been nice had we known where you were."

I say, "And Walter."

"Walter? The Hells Angel? What were you doing with Walter?"

"Planning our next big ride. C'mon Pop, he's not a Hells Angel. We ran into him at Revel."

He sets his jaw.

Marvin sits on the end of the couch, nose buried in a book, which he closes with a *pop!* and says, "Bedtime."

Smart boy, and I take his cue. "Pop, can we do this tomorrow?

"What will be different tomorrow?"

I don't know, Pop your better angel will visit in your sleep. "Maybe they'll find Frankie." I walk toward my room, avoiding all the ways this conversation could go bad.

I'm staring at what would be the ceiling if it weren't so dark in here, voices from this crazy day fading in and out, struggling to make sense of all that doesn't, when a sliver of light cuts across the ceiling. "Hey. You awake?"

"Yeah, Marvin. I'm awake."

"Can I come in?"

He sits on the end of the bed. "I'm really sorry about Dad," he says.

I say, "He's not your fault."

"Yeah, but I should stand up for you when he attacks like that. I always bail."

"There's nothing you could say that would make it one bit different."

"How about, 'Why is everything about *you*, Dad?' Or, 'Why aren't you hurting for Frankie?'" He sighs. "Do you think he's . . . "

"Dead?"

He grunts like someone kicked him. "Yeah."

"I can't let myself think that. Everyone there saw more than I did. I came out of the water to all kinds of crazy."

"I was mean to him."

"Don't you think like that, either. Frankie's really hard, Marvin. Everyone gets irritated with him."

"Yeah, but I knew that. I knew he couldn't *help* it, like, he has *obsessions*. You can't be mean when you know stuff."

"Marvin, whatever was going on with Frankie was about Sheila and the rest of my weird-ball family. He likes you and me better than anybody. You think he would have played like he was playing the other day when I snuck up on you guys, if he was within a hundred miles of Sheila? Or any of her so-called boyfriends?"

"I guess . . . "

"And stop talking about him in the past tense. Us being

afraid he's dead doesn't mean he is. Cops are banging down doors of all the registered sex offenders in town; they're the ones that usually kill kids. It's been all over TV that anyone in the park who took pictures or videos on their phones should contact the police. *Some*body had to think of YouTube with all that going on."

"But the longer he's gone . . . "

"Stop. Okay?"

He's on the end of the bed with his back to me and I hear him sniffle as he gets up to walk out. *Dang!* "Come here."

"I'm okay."

"Come *here*."

He comes back and sits next to me on the edge of the bed. I pull back the covers and push him down beside me, put my arms around him from behind. "Sleep here," I whisper. "We'll both feel better."

CHAPTER
TEN

"So now you can say you slept with a girl," I tell Marvin at breakfast.

"Do I get to brag?"

"If you want a fat lip to go with your fat head."

Pop is at work and Momma is upstairs getting ready to go to hers.

"What are you doing today?"

"Passing out fliers for Frankie later," he says. "First I've got three lawns to mow, but that shouldn't take too long. How about you?"

Marvin shames me when it comes to the world of work. He doesn't just mow lawns; he's like a full-care lawn service. He pulls this makeshift trailer behind his bike, with his lawnmower and an edger and a hedge trimmer. I filled out the application for a job cleaning up at the multiplex when I turned sixteen, but Pop thought he could finally talk me into turning out for club basketball and the application was never turned in. At some point I need to kick the employment thing into gear. If I had my own money, Pop would have less control.

"The police asked me to stop by so I'm headed over there, then over to social services," I say now.

"Whoa. You scared?"

"Why would I be scared?"

"You know; they might ask questions that put your family in a bad light, Sheila at least."

"My family doesn't need me to shine light on them, bad or any other kind. They shine their own lights."

"Why are you going to social services?"

"Mr. Novotny asked me if I could stop in. That's cool; he's one of the good guys for sure."

Marvin places his spoon in his cereal bowl. "What can *I* do?" He seems . . . desperate.

"Marvin, we're just gonna have to feel this way until something happens."

"You'll let me know, though, right? Like if they think of a new place to search where kids can be of assistance?"

I hold up my phone. "You're at the top of my contacts."

He rolls his eyes. "Contacts are alphabetical." He stares at his cereal.

"The Quakers went to a lot of trouble to make that," I say. "Eat."

He sinks his spoon in.

"Then go do your fliers and make the neighborhood neat and green again."

Marvin finishes his oats, places his bowl in the sink, and starts for the garage to get his mower. "Listen," he says at the door, "thanks. For last night. I was afraid of my impending dreams."

Impending dreams. "Welcome to my life," I say. "Anytime."

"I can sleep with you anytime?" Marvin is getting his sense of humor back.

"Go forth and mow."

"Your sister's a piece of work," Officer Graham says.

I say, "Half sister."

"Bet you wish it was a smaller fraction," he says. "At any rate we're hoping people who know her can fill in some blanks. What's the best way to get in touch with her mother?"

"Create an app where you can get rich blaming other people for your crappy life."

He smiles.

"And if you think my *sister* is a piece of work . . . "

"Apple and tree?" he says, then catches himself. "I'm sorry. That was . . . "

"You'll have to work harder than that to offend me," I tell him. "Yeah, apple and tree. That apple didn't fall. I fell and *rolled*."

"You were in the pool when your nephew disappeared?"

"Uh-huh. Embarrassing as it is, I'm the reason everyone was there."

"How so?"

"My entourage," I say. "Or *entourages*. I have followers from both the Montagues and the Capulets. They were all there to watch me swim."

"You must be a pretty good swimmer."

"Let's don't go there."

He nods. "So you had a different point of view from the others."

"I did, but I never saw Frankie. By the time I finished my race, the chaos was on."

"We talked to the librarian and some of the kids from your book club," he says. "She was helpful to the point that she could be. She said you all had been reading a book about a swimmer, so they all came to watch you."

"Yeah. The swimmer in the book is the exact opposite of me."

He writes in his notebook. "I understand Frankie spent quite a bit of time with your foster parents, the Howards?"

"My sister used to bring him . . . *brings* him over when she's headed out to do other-than-motherly things," I say. "It's her way of staying out of the line of fire of CPS."

"They have no problem taking him?"

"No. I mean, they've got *me*, and I can get him to behave—well, *kind of* behave—when I'm home. Plus, he likes my foster mom; and their son . . . my foster brother."

He puts down his notebook. "Do you have suspicions? Any gut-level stuff, fears gnawing in the back of your mind?"

"Maybe one . . . kind of a general one. My sister had this asshole boyfriend—a guy named Butch—carbon copy of the last ten. I saw a pretty nasty bruise on Frankie's arm that I think he put there, like he punched him. He's supposedly gone now, but my sister gets into relationships with these weak, angry guys who are usually afraid of her."

Officer Graham says, "That's interesting. . . . "

"Yeah. Most of them, except for this last guy, Butch, would be afraid to fight her, like, *physically*, but I've never seen her with a guy she wasn't trying to humiliate. Maybe one of them decided to get even."

"That's a stretch," he says, "but worth looking into. We didn't think to ask her specifically about past boyfriends. Maybe we can get some names."

"If she can remember them."

"Can you help us with any?"

"No," I say. "I've always stayed away; I get way too mad. Of course, if you have a list of small-time drug dealers who live with their mothers . . . "

"Look, Annie, we're trying to move fast on this. We know timetables. If you think of anything else, call. Except for the librarian and your foster parents, you're the sanest person I've talked to." He hands me his card.

"The old guy who was here yesterday, the guy with all the tats? Name's Walter?" I say. "Put him toward the top of your 'sane' list."

"Noted. Thanks again."

I close my eyes. "Do you think . . . "

"I don't think on these," he says, and touches my shoulder, "and you shouldn't either. There are a lot of possibilities, and not all of them are bad. I promise we'll do everything we can. Most of the men and women on the force have families; they take this personally."

～ ～ ～

"Annie! How long . . . "

"Hey, Mr. Novotny . . . "

"If you don't want me to call you Miss Boots, you best start using my first name. When you were little the Howards thought they were teaching you manners making you call me that, but you've been off my caseload since your mom's rights were terminated, and—I don't know a good way to say this—manners have never been your strong suit. So, Wiz, okay?"

"Wiz it izzz."

"Okay. That's settled. Frankie. You guys must be going crazy."

"You can't *go* where you already *are*."

He snorts, in recognition. "How's Sheila?"

"If you've been watching TV, you know she's busy rewriting history."

He grunts. "Annie, did we blow this one?"

"We?"

"The department. What all do you know? Should we have gotten Frankie out of there? I know he's not an open case, but only because Sheila knows when she's going off the deep end, she can keep us off her back by getting him someplace safe. Which has been to the Howards'. Have you guys seen anything?"

I don't know what's safe to say. Whatever happened to

Frankie, it wasn't Sheila's *intention,* and as angry as I am, if he isn't found or if he's found—I can't even say it—I don't want her living the rest of her life thinking she's the only reason, even though she kind of is. I *hate* the way my mind goes back and forth about her. And Nancy.

Wiz must see my reluctance. "This is all off the record, okay? I'm writing nothing down and no one's in trouble. I'm going to assume Frankie will be found soon, and I need to know where to point my caseworker."

"Your caseworker?"

He points to the door. "Read the sign. I'm a supervisor now. This is where the buck stops. I've got Jeff Humphries from the *Review* speed-dialing me every fifteen minutes. Far as he's concerned, child protection services is a euphemism."

I say, "A supervisor, huh? Wow, what did you *do*?"

Wiz laughs. "I was in the restroom when they were overhauling our division."

"You should have held it."

"You don't know the half of it."

"But you said *your caseworker.* Frankie didn't have a caseworker."

"He will. We had an anonymous call a few weeks back that didn't make it through Intake—not enough specifics. With his disappearance, it will. I'd like to do a little insider trading so we know which direction to go. What can you tell me?"

"He had this big bruise, really black," I say. "I should have said something, but I went over and threatened Sheila instead. If Frankie gets removed, the Howards won't take him full-time, 'cause of Pop, which means he'd lose everyone. And what other foster home is going to take him? Plus, as much of an unconscious bitch as my sister is, two days away from her and Frankie is totally off the wall, trying to get home. You know how that goes."

"Yeah. A bruise, no matter how black, wouldn't have gotten him out. Look, I know enough about your family that when something bad happens, drugs or alcohol—or both—are involved. If you carry any weight with your sister, tell her to get into treatment *pronto*; get off TV and get clean.

Sometimes I think Mr. Novotny—*Wiz*—saved my life. I know he couldn't have spent as much time with all of the kids on his caseload as he did with me, but he could get me to straighten up when my therapists or the school or the Howards were ready to throw in the towel. He's one of those guys willing to break a rule if it looks like a dumb one. He'd always say, "Annie, let's look at what we want to make happen, and make it happen." That's where Sheila has to get right now.

August 24— Session #Who's Counting?
ANNIE BOOTS

Came in distraught over the disappearance of her sister's son. Newspaper account attached. Dressed in shorts and athletic T-shirt, looking tired and drawn.

Annie: I guess you know all about it.

Me: Of course. I'm so sorry, Annie. What have you heard?

Annie: Almost nothing. It's crazy; everything was right out in the open, people all over the park, and Frankie just disappeared.

Me: That is crazy. So what do you want to talk about?

Annie: (looks at me like I'm an idiot)

Me: My bad. I know what, but what can we do in here to help you?

Annie: It feels like my fault. I mean, I know I didn't have anything to do with whatever actually happened to him, but all those people were there because of me being in that stupid swim meet and I know how dangerous a life Frankie lives because of my sister and the guys she hangs out with and . . . just with the company she keeps and how she doesn't pay attention.

Me: Tell me what you think you could have done to keep this from happening, and I mean from what you knew at the time.

Annie: I spend all my time trying to keep my lives apart; you know, the one I come from and the one I live in, and the minute I'm not paying attention, they come together. If that stupid fight had never broken out, none of this would have happened, and the common denominator in that fight was me.

Me: That's one way to put it together, but it seems like a stretch. Let's stop and take a breath. Look back at what you and I have gone over so many times. What is the one thing you do that gives you the most grief?

Annie: (sighs and falls back in the chair) Try to control everything. Spend too much energy trying to make people believe something that isn't true.

Me: About . . .

Annie: About what I'm doing as opposed to how I'm feeling.

Me: And . . .

Annie: It feels good when it's working, and really really shitty when it isn't.

Me: And . . .

Annie: It always ends up feeling really really shitty.

Me: So, you're really mad, and feeling awful, about not controlling something you had no idea was going to happen, even after you knew you had no business trying to control it in the first place. Let's talk about what's really going on.

Annie: (choking) What if he's dead? Or what if he's somewhere awful wondering why nobody's coming to save him. I'm supposed to be the one who saves him. (falls into my arms and lays there for the rest of the session.)

Impression: Obvious

Emily Palmer, M.A.

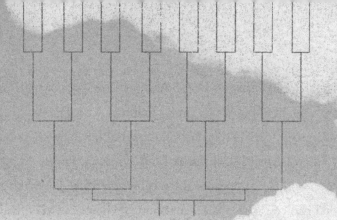

CHAPTER
ELEVEN

Time supposedly heals all wounds, but I think the saying should be time heals *clean* wounds. Frankie's disappearance is jagged. He's been gone three weeks and there's been *nothing*. If he isn't alive—if we *knew* he isn't alive—we could know how to feel. But no matter how long he's gone, it just sneaks up on you that he might be somewhere in big trouble wondering why nobody who loves him will come. You see this stuff on TV all the time, but when it's someone you know, it attacks your *imagination*.

That's where Frankie is for me, and my imagination can be a horrifying place.

But whether time heals wounds or not, it does march on.

(There are so many clichés about time it makes me want to throw up, but I don't have time.) And now school has started, and on the surface I'm just another hotshot jock cranking up my volleyball season where I can win some games, do my schoolwork, and appear to responsible adults like I'm making good choices. Basketball is my sport of choice but volleyball is a good warm-up.

There's no manipulating games during the season. You can take the other team out in three games or stretch it to five, but there's no time in between for socializing, and these days all bets are off with Pop and the Boots anyway, because as far as he's concerned their presence on the planet is a curse, and with Frankie gone the whole Boots unit, such as it is, is more fractured. Nancy showed up with Walter for our first exhibition game, but I only waved toward the stands when I caught her eye.

Officer Graham makes contact every week just to say there's been no progress, so the whole ugly mess sits as far back in my mind as I can push it, filed under "Shit You Can't Do Anything About."

And because my life seems only to progress on the wings of conflict, Pop and I stay locked in unpleasantness.

I came in after the match tonight—which we won in straight games—chucked my duffel into the corner, and plopped onto the couch. Momma had the TV on one of those reality shows that is anything but real. In this one the contestants are all wannabe singers getting judged by real singers so they, too, can become real singers. By real singers I mean those who make a lot of money. To my untrained ear, it sounds like some of the contestants are already better than the real ones, only no big bucks. I hate this show because every time someone gets picked, someone else doesn't. Whoever doesn't acts like they're really grateful for the opportunity to have worked with one of their true heroes and to have had the chance to perform on the national stage. Hey, statistically there's no way one of those four superstars is the *one* the losing contestant grew up wanting to be just like, so that part's a crock; and there's *no* way the person is that grateful right after not being picked. I mean, I don't care how far up the ladder I've made it, if you have the chance to pick me and you don't, I hate your guts.

"So how do you grade yourself on tonight's match?" Pop got straight As all the way through high school and college. He's a big fan of the alphabet.

This is an irritating conversation we have after every one of my sporting events, excluding swimming, of course, where we both happily give me an F. It's easier when we get into it over *school* grades, because I can fall back on whatever the teacher gave me. The problem with *this* conversation is, if I give myself an A he points out the physical errors or lapses in judgment he believes should put at least a minus after that, and if I give myself something lower than an A, he wants to know what I could have done to bring it up. That's the long way of saying Pop likes to tell me what I did wrong. After all, Michael Jordan was never satisfied, right?

"I don't know, Pop," I say, hoping beyond all experience that for once I could hit the letter on the head, "a B maybe? B plus?"

"You know there was a scout there from Eastern, right?"

"Uh-huh."

"I sat with her."

"Was she cute?"

Out of the corner of my eye, I see Momma smile. If this gets too hairy, she'll take my side.

Pop says, "I see. You're not going to take this seriously."

I take a deep breath. "C'mon, that was funny. If I get recruited, it'll be for basketball anyway." Then I bite. "So what grade did the Eastern scout give me?"

"She was more interested in Hannah," he says. "They're looking for a good setter. Seemed like she set up Mariah more than you tonight."

"Well, she's got no shot at Hannah," I tell him. "She's

WSU all the way. Her parents and older sister were all Cougs."

"You might want to get on her good side."

"C'mon Pop, Mariah was on fire tonight."

"But everyone knows she's shooting for the Naval Academy."

"We play to win, not to get recruited." I mumble it.

"Excuse me?"

"Nothing. There will be plenty of chances for scouts. None of them would have even been here if it weren't for Hannah and Mariah. I'm *basketball*, Pop."

Pop crosses his arms and I'm about to hear how excellence is excellence no matter the endeavor when Momma steps in. "Could you two table this?" She nods toward the monster flat screen mounted above the fireplace.

"Yeah," I say, pointing at that same screen, "these people are all about excellence."

Most of what I hear about the Boots comes from Walter, who tells of Nancy's mood swings and rantings about Sheila's motherly failings, and Sheila's creative name-calling.

Walter and I have been meeting at Revel 77 about once a week. He seems kind of worn down, but he always shows and either Leah or I always pay, and it's always interesting.

"You good for another cup?"

Leah and I are both reading, and I gaze up out of the fog. "You're still following me."

"Guilty."

I squint. "You reporting to anyone?"

"Like your mother? Lord no," he says. "If she knew we were getting together, she'd accuse me of hitting on you."

I wish that were a surprise.

Leah says, "Tell her you're hitting on *me*. I have a thing for older bikers."

Walter laughs. "There's a difference between older bikers and *old* bikers," he says. "Before you act on that *thing*, you'd do well to learn that difference."

I'm between practice and dinner, reading *Grayson,* the crazy cold water swimmer lady's follow-up to *Swimming to Antarctica.* Walter glances at the cover. "Good book?"

"Leah's recommendation."

She smiles and waves without looking up from her book.

He nods toward me. "Have you seen Sheila?"

"Not for a while. Now that there's no Frankie, we don't cross paths much. She's gotta know I'm mad enough to skin her alive. Why?"

"I don't know; for a minute there with all the TV attention, I thought she'd actually try to pull things together, but I only see her at your mom's place these days, and she's dropping weight fast. . . . "

I say, "Like a meth user?"

"Exactly like that."

"She still got teeth?"

"Don't be mean," he says.

I watch him across the table. Leather vest over a raggedy T-shirt, Levi's but no boots—Converse All-Stars—clean, gray shoulder-length hair, a book peeking over the top of his saddle bag on the floor next to his helmet, coffee steaming in the cup. I have to ask again. "Walter, what are you doing mixed up with my family? You're way better than that. I mean, you're a good-looking guy. Smart. You're so kind it scares me. How do you put up with the craziness, my sister's nastiness?"

He looks over at our reflection in the window. "I am a pretty good-lookin' fella, aren't I?"

"Yeah, you are."

He looks a little longer. "What I am is a pretty good-lookin' *old* fella," he says. Then back at me. "Old enough to know your sister never got enough time to take a breath, step back, and see what was happenin' to her so she could stop herself from making it happen to the next one down. I know how she got bounced around, how she was treated in some of those places, and how it was no better most times when she came home. That girl's lucky to be alive, if that passes for luck. Point is, if I was Sheila, I'd be lookin' around for someone I could vent my rage on, too. Rather see her like that than hopeless; when she gets like that, she could do damage to herself."

I say, "Maybe, but when she makes her crazy accusations and calls *you* old and irrelevant, and Nancy every name in the book, it has to get old."

He smiles. "That's the good news about old age and hearing."

Leah closes her binder over her book and rises. "Gotta do it, you guys. Tonight's family night and I missed the last two."

Walter watches her go. "I checked that girl out on the sports page. She as quick in the water as everyone says?"

"Quicker," I say. "Works out ten thousand meters a day, minimum."

"Whew! Wish I still had *that* kind of energy."

"You might if you weren't wasting so much of it on Nancy."

"Your mom's life looks different to me than to you."

"Walter, I've seen Nancy from about every angle there is, and it just can't be easy. I know she has her days, but she can be meaner than a snake."

"And how do you think she got so mean?"

"Probably the same way most people get mean," I say. "From getting treated bad."

"Bad treatment's a soul killer," he says, and squints, breathes deep. "I probably shouldn't tell you this."

I nod toward his empty cup. "Buy you another cup of coffee if you do."

"Deal," he says slowly, "but you got to swear to secrecy. I mean *swear*. You knowin' this would kill your mother. *Anybody* knowin' it would kill her."

I get his refill.

"I've known Nancy even longer than you think," he says. "Long time ago I was in treatment with her."

"You're an addict?"

"Naw, drugs never did much for me. Smoked some weed in 'Nam, but pretty much anything else made me feel out of control, and that's not my thing."

"So what were you doing in a treatment program?"

"Benefits," he says. "Government was right there to thank you for your service when you're hunkered down in war, but that was about all the *thank you* you'd get unless you had something wrong you could prove. You coulda been sprayed with chemicals that'd take the skin right off you, and cauterize your lungs in the process, but if you couldn't *prove* your condition was a result of that damn war, the G-Men just put you on hold. They finally came across with some bennies for the guys they bathed in Agent Orange, but not before a whole lot of them died waiting. Drug addict was the easiest. All you had to do was get a doc to say the word, and if you knew what you were doing you could get in a program, get on housing, get a Pell Grant if your GI Bill was used up. If they didn't have a viable VA program in your area, you could get into a local one. It's better these days, I guess."

"So you went into drug treatment even though you weren't an addict."

"Not too hard to get off drugs when you're not on 'em. But what I couldn't get off was that damn war."

"A lot of bad stuff happen to you?"

"A lot of bad stuff happened to everyone," he says. "That wasn't what was killing me. It was what I'd done."

"What did you do?"

"Let's just say, things that are hard to forgive, things that sneak up on you later."

"PTSD?"

"Call it what you want."

"So then . . . "

"I'd tried everything. Went to church, did about every damn risky thing I could think of that might kill me, meditated; I just got more confused. Every church told me something different—

didn't know whether to let Jesus save me or save myself. Couldn't figure good from bad, love from hate. Went decades like that. One night around midnight I rode over to the Monroe Street bridge thinking about going out the easy way. Was actually sitting with my legs over the edge when I got it: if I jump and there's a god, I'm going to have to account for myself."

"For jumping?"

"Naw, I'd have just said 'Hell with you, Lord, you made it too hard.' Don't know why I hadn't thought of this before; I just needed to save as many lives as I took. I didn't know how many I took, but I knew I'd ruined a bunch of them. My government talked me into going to a place I had no right going, doing things I had no right doing."

The clock above the counter says I'm late for dinner, but I'm *not* interrupting this.

"Came down off that bridge," he says. "Rode to a meeting, decided that was as good a place as any to find some of those particular lives. Turned out, the only person can save a person is *that person*, but I found I could be a help sometimes; you know, shut my mouth and listen, be a witness. Did that off and on for *years*. Then one night when you were just a pup, I run into Nancy. She was new . . . think you had just been taken again and she was *raw*, stress so great she looked to be bleeding out the eyes, nearly twice as big as she is now; obese to the point you could hear her breathing clear across the room. I remember thinking, *This woman's gonna stroke out before this meeting starts*. She made it through, but she was one miserable drug-crazed lady. Ugly and desperate as her life looked, it seemed like there was a light in there somewhere, felt familiar somehow. So I took it as a test."

"A test. Like . . . *God* testing you?"

"The *world* tests you, Annie. If there's a god, he has bigger fish to fry. Anyway, we start talking. Hell, she was the victim of every-damn-thing. Protective services lying to her, stealing her babies when they got no right. Ungrateful kids, asshole boyfriends. Pretty much anything negative invented in the world was tracking Nancy Boots."

"Did you tell her to grow up?"

"Told her no such thing," he says. "I listened. You challenge somebody laying out their troubles, all you're doing is giving them reasons to think harder on what they're already thinking, and setting it up so they won't listen when you *do* have something to say. Adds to their ammo, if you know what I mean. You can't help *any*body unless you're willing to hear their story." He smiles and winks at me. "So stop asking questions and listen to mine."

I smile back. And zip it.

"Couple meetings later we're on break and I'm standing in the lobby after taking a leak; hear this, this . . . *sobbing* from inside the ladies' room. Then these two women come out all horrified and laughing, and as the door's closing I hear the sobbing again. The two women walk away shaking their heads and elbowing each other and I'm thinking, only other person I saw go in was Nancy. I wait a bit and no one else comes out, so in I go, hear more crying coming from one of the stalls. I ask if everyone's okay in there and the sobbing stops, but I don't get an answer. I ask, 'Is that you, Nancy Boots?' and it's quiet a second, then this weak 'Yeah,' so what the hell, I open the door and there's your momma sittin' with a roll of paper in her hand. I say, 'What's wrong?' and she just looks at me. I say 'What's *wrong?*' and she bursts into tears again, says, 'My arms are too short.'"

Oh my god, Nancy got so heavy she couldn't reach around . . . she couldn't clean herself.

"Those women were laughing at *her*. I'm furious; I mean, killing mad. So I help your mom out and we get ready to go back to the meeting, but she says, 'I can't go back there,' and I say, 'If you can't, I can't,' and take her to my car, go back inside, stand in front of those bitches, and say, 'You ladies can get clean and sober all you want—never *touch* another drug—but you still won't have a bit of damn decency.' Last meeting I ever went to."

"Wow, Walter. You got together with Nancy wiping her. . . ."

His hand shoots up. "You don't need that movie in your

head, and I don't need the rerun. Point is, we're sitting in the car and she's still crying and thanking me for getting her out of there, and I see a big ol' woman with a right pretty face, if you can see past her life. Maybe it was timing, but I'd done plenty of things in *my* life that left an ache on someone, so I thought the two of us might have a project."

I have *never* seen Nancy as pretty. I've seen her big and I've seen her relatively small, seen rage and revenge and hurt written all over her, but never pretty.

"I told you before, this part isn't for you. You grow up with someone as up and down as Nancy's been over the years, you got to take care of yourself; I get that. You're doin' it. This other part's my duty. I'm just sayin' . . . I could only help her heal if I was ready to heal myself."

I rub my eyes, look at him. "You thought she was pretty."

"I knew damn well she was pretty. Hell, how do you think you got to looking like you do? That Rance fella's no prize."

We sit awhile, watching people move in and out, set up their laptops.

I'm overdue at home, so I pack my stuff into my backpack and stand up with him. "Keep following me, Walter."

He nods, puts a hand on my shoulder. I move his hand and hug him. "You're a great guy, Walter. Kind of like a saint."

"Long damn way from that."

Cool thing about book club; it goes year-round. Sharon is not fond of the fact that schools work hard to make sure we don't read anything we can fall in love with, so she does her best to work around our schedules.

"I just read a chapter of a book we should consider," Leah says. She holds it up. "*Living Dead Girl.* Elizabeth Scott."

Maddy says, "Zombies?"

"*Way* not zombies," Leah says. "It's about this cool little tough ten-year-old girl who gets kidnapped by a pedophile. First night, he parks with her across from her home and describes in great detail what he'll do to every member of her family if she tries to get away. He knows all their names. She tells the story as a teenager, still his captive."

I say, "*Jesus,* Leah."

"That's right," she says. "I'm doing it for you. Worst thing you can do when bad things happen is dance around them. Making yourself tough is never the wrong thing. Ask Lynne Cox."

Maddy says, "Cold water and losing . . . they're not the same."

"Body and mind," Leah says. "One in the same. Ask. Lynne. Cox."

The very thought of reading the book she just described

makes my stomach churn, but in a strange way, tugs at me.

Sharon glances toward me. "It's a good book, but every bit as disturbing as good. I have to put a warning label on this one."

"For me," I say.

"For you," she says.

"Well, you're right. It's killing me. But I gotta go with Leah. And Lynne Cox."

Sharon rolls her eyes and throws up her hands. She's funny.

I'm curled up on the couch in the basement rec room watching an installment of this *very* strange cable TV series called *The Leftovers*. The premise is that on October 14 of whatever year, at the exact same moment, two percent of the population of Earth *vanished*. That's two out of every one hundred people, so no matter who you are, you lost somebody or somebody close to you has. If you were in a car with a driver who disappeared, you better get your foot over to the brake. If you were some guy making love with one of the two percent, you better be on a soft mattress because you're going to fall about a foot. Farther if it happened to be Nancy. At any rate, it seems everything I run into these days is about loss. Marvin is playing a video game on his computer and watching out of the corner of his eye. As much of a control freak as Pop is, he doesn't use Parental Controls and these "leftover" people screw like rabbits, because who knows when it will happen again. I'll bet Marvin is hitting all-time lows on his game scores.

My iPhone pings.

Walter: Meet me for coffee

Me: When

Walter: Now

Me: On my way.

I say, "Marvin, memorize the naked scenes. There'll be a test."

"Which I will pass with flying colors. I may even go on the Internet afterward to pick up some extra credit."

And I'm off to Revel.

"Sheila's gone," Walter says as I join him at the back table.

"Where?"

He shrugs. "If I knew that, I'd have said so. After your mom and Sheila's last tangle, Sheila quit coming over. Nancy got to feeling bad for her part in it and sent me to see if I could coax her to come for dinner. Place was empty."

"No Yvonne either?"

He shakes his head. "I'm worried. The girl's got *nothing*

going. She's gotta figure when Frankie comes back, he's going straight into the system. That mess on his arm by itself wouldn't have gotten anything but a warning, but the case is high-profile now with all the damn TV and your family history. The fact that he disappeared out from under her nose along with her current free-fallin' weight loss . . . . three strikes." Walter still talks like there's no chance Frankie won't show up.

My stomach jumps. The other side of Sheila's rage is hopelessness. "You think she'll hurt herself?"

"I would."

I close my eyes. "I guess I might, too. Does Nancy know Sheila's gone?"

"Not yet." He scratches the week's growth on his chin. "One other thing. I'm not gonna tell you quite yet, but . . . do you think you could get me an audience with that old caseworker of yours?"

"An audience?"

"Fancy word for a talk."

"I know what an audience is, Walter," and I laugh. "It's what I get with you every week or so right here. Why do you want to talk to Wiz?

"All will be revealed, young lady. All will be revealed."

~ ~ ~

We're wrapping up our book club session on *Living Dead Girl* and I'm glad. This story is the kind of fiction that's truer than truth, because of what it does inside your head. Sharon was right to warn me about it, Leah was right to bring it, and I was right to read it; it set me up for anything. It doesn't end the way I'd like, but enough is enough.

Mark says, "It reminds me of that guy who kidnapped the three girls back in the early two-thousands. He kept them until, like, two-thousand-thirteen."

"Ariel Castro," Sharon says. "He went to prison. Committed suicide there."

"Kidnap, suicide," Seth says. "Unfortunate he didn't reverse the order."

"So why is this book so powerful?" Sharon asks, holding up her copy. "Anyone think it wasn't?"

Nobody thinks that.

Oscar says it was so powerful he didn't read past the first chapter. "Too real. Where I come from . . . Too real."

"I believe you," Sharon says, "which takes me back to my original question."

"Stories get into your head in a way the real world doesn't," Leah says. "When you read about that Castro guy, you think about what it must have been like for those girls, like how *trapped* they were and how they couldn't know the truth about anything going on right on the outer walls of that house, and it's bad but it's over at the time you're hearing about it and everyone's okay; well, maybe not okay, but alive and getting help. But when you read a story like *Living Dead Girl,* you walk with her, page by page, like in real time, and you have no idea whether or not everything's going to be okay."

"Yeah," I say. "You're with her. You could *be* her."

Layton gives a short laugh. "You know how the best review a book can get is supposed to be, 'I couldn't put it down'? Well, I couldn't *not* put this one down. But then I couldn't *not* pick it back up."

Maddy starts to talk, then chokes. "You know what I hated? I hated that she was such a cool kid before he got her, and then she was just more and more scooped out."

That sends my heart into my throat.

Up goes Seth's hand. The one outlier. "It was a good book," he says. "Held together well. I thought the author was a superb word conservationist. But this *power* you all seem to have succumbed to eluded me."

Sharon says, "And we know why that is, don't we, Seth?"

"We know the theory," Seth says.

"But it's a theory like evolution, don't you think? Like . . . solid?"

"Maybe pretty solid," Seth admits.

"C'mon, buddy, you got to give me this one," Sharon says. "You have the big figure-it-out brain. The rational brain. These babies . . . "—and her hand sweeps the group—"have the big crybaby brain, the emotional one. Your emotional brain is, like, one-celled."

"A bit of hyperbole," Seth says, "but you're the librarian, so I'll concede that."

Sharon slaps both palms on the table. "Good! You guys know what's next, right? We all agreed? Four weeks telling our *own* stories. Remember? We tell them, then we write them."

There is a grudging, collective, "Yeah . . . "

"Hey," she says, "it's a writer's club, too, and lately we've been doing way more reading than writing."

This has always seemed like the most dangerous part of this club to me; it requires *way* more trust than I'm used to allowing.

Up goes Seth's hand, again. "I don't believe I had a voice in this decision. Is there a reason I wasn't informed about this aspect?"

"There is," Sharon says. "When your mother called to inquire about this club, she told me you'd be resistant, that self-disclosure isn't your thing; so we agreed to be honorable. We kept it from you."

"Did you have conversations with *everyone's* mother before bringing them in?"

"No," she says. "Everyone else joined without assistance from their mother."

Seth nods in surrender, shows us the closest thing he knows to embarrassment with a head shake and a glance toward the ground. "I guess my mother and I need to have another conversation."

Seth doesn't realize how much he's disclosing, telling us there were *other* conversations.

"And *why* would talking about one's life have anything to do with one's writing anyway?" He seems indignant.

"Good stories *come* from life," Sharon says. "And for most writers, it's the easiest place to start."

"Well, it seems like an outlandish waste of time to me, if you want the truth."

"I don't want the truth, Seth. Nobody's going to make you tell your story, but if you listen you might understand why the rest of us will." She keeps looking at Seth, but the rest is catch-up for us. "See, life happens as much in the imagination as it does out where there's earth, wind, and fire. How we *understand* story can be a blueprint for understanding our lives. Things happen in seemingly random order, but if we pay attention to real events the way an author pays attention to story, we're forced to look at *cause and effect*, and understanding cause and effect shows us the *relatedness* of events, and our parts in them."

"If more teachers knew that," Maddy says, "we wouldn't be reading so much *shit* in our English classes."

"But if you weren't reading so much shit in your English classes, I'd have a harder time getting you to my book club, so be nice to your English teachers. And read the *shit* they give you. Some of it is really good shit. Now, any storytellers?"

Mark says, "This is crazy. I have this . . . I don't know, almost a compulsion to say something, but it's swimming around in my head in a way . . . that makes it hard to find, like, the *opening paragraph*."

Sharon says, "Remember in our last writing block, we decided it's not necessary to start at the 'start,' that you jump in at the most compelling part."

Mark shifts around in his seat and he stares into that "nowhere" space a few inches in front of him, and he looks like he's about to jump into water only Lynne Cox could endure. "You guys scare the heck out of me . . . I mean, this *club*.

"Yet here you are," Maddy says.

"Yeah. Here I am. So here goes. I go to church; my whole family does. We believe what we hear, try to act on those beliefs. As long as we do that, everything is calm at our house. But I have an older sister; she was my hero because she always took me with her, and looked out for me when I did stupid things. She taught me to hunt, to never pull the trigger without a clear shot, never kill something for the fun of killing. My whole family does that, but I was Stella's *project*, and she made sure I did good and felt good."

What I wouldn't give for an older sister like that.

"But then she got pregnant. Our church is pro-life—zero tolerance on that one. Stella was seventeen. She had plans for college and a career and though she *thought* she was pro-life, it turned out she wasn't. Long story short, she had an abortion and, on my mother's orders, was banished. It is *forbidden* to mention her name. Anyone caught contacting her risks the exact same punishment. My *story*, I guess, is about a guy who had no problem believing what people who loved him told him, until he realized what that could cost. I ache every day. I go to sleep every night wondering if Stella hates me because, after all she did for me, I turned away."

"And to double down on the plot," I say, before I even realize I'm talking, "if you do go to her, you lose seven other people, all family."

Mark massages his forehead. "And Jesus," he says finally.

"Let's hold off on Jesus," Layton says. "As our fearless leader has always said, *To Kill a Mockingbird* is a whole different story if Boo Radley tells it. See, I go to church, too, and the Jesus I know would treat your mother like a money changer, no offense to your mother."

"No offense to money changers," Leah says.

Up goes the hand of Seth. "*So*, you start your story with the abortion, tell half of it in flashbacks, and fix the ending in a way that suits you. Who's next?"

Mark bursts out laughing.

Sharon's face is in her hands. When it comes up you can see she had the same reaction as Mark. "As abrupt and devoid of empathy as that may have sounded," she says, "Seth might be onto something. Almost all writers will tell you they struggle with endings. The one they think they were working toward suddenly doesn't work because of unexpected events that snuck into the story. Sometimes those unexpected events make the author think maybe she or he doesn't *know* enough to tell that story, that more research is needed, either life research or library research. In the end, the more they discover—the more they *know*—guides them toward a truthful ending. By that I mean an ending that could really happen."

Oscar says, "What are you saying?"

"I'm saying it's possible Mark doesn't know enough yet to bring his story home. It's possible he sees the same choices Annie sees. But it's *also* possible there are outcomes he hasn't thought of because he doesn't know about them, and maybe this is one of those stories he puts in a folder, while he catches up."

"And," Layton says, "as our Divine Librarian might say, Mark is not only the author of this story, he's the author of his life."

Sharon gives her knowing nod.

"Which means," I say, not without a sense of personal irony, "if he changes his life, the story could go with it."

A tear runs down Marks cheek.

Sharon says, "And Mark can't leave the story in the folder too long because Stella needs to read it."

It's after midnight when my head hits the pillow, having obsessed most of the evening on Mark. I swear, family pulls through impenetrable barriers, barriers that seem to leave us no good choices. I picture his mother *banishing* (God, I hate that word) his sister from the family and I'm actually grateful I have an ignorant narrow-minded mother rather than a smart narrow-minded one.

Sweet dreams, Annie Boots.

CHAPTER
TWELVE

"Really like to thank you for meeting with me," Walter says, extending his hand.

"Any friend of Annie's . . . " Wiz says.

" . . . is usually a pain in the butt," I say before he can finish. "But this is different."

Wiz says, "That's because most of your friends are at an age where they couldn't *possibly* be bearers of good news."

"I don't know about good news," Walter says. "But I do have news."

"At this point," Wiz says, "almost any news would be good. Swear this department is buried . . . in caseloads, in paperwork and . . . what . . . an incapacity to help kids." He shakes his head as if to throw out cobwebs. "Sorry, Mr. . . . "

"Call me Walter."

"You have news."

Walter nods slowly, glances sideways at me. "I know where Frankie Boots is."

In unison, Wiz and me: "What?"

My first thought: "Is he . . . ?"

"He's fine," Walter says. "And safe. Has been all along."

I'm *stupefied*! "Where? When did . . . "

Wiz puts up a hand. "Annie. Let the man talk. Go ahead, Walter. Where is he?"

"I've got him," Walter says.

"Where did you find him?"

"I took him."

Wiz sits forward. "What?"

"I took him," Walter says. "From the park."

The two men look at each other in silence for a sec, while I try to close my mouth.

"I came to see the swim contest," Walter says. "I was tagging behind talking to a guy wearing one of those vet's baseball caps when the craziness broke out. I saw the boy running in circles with his fingers in his ears, hollerin' like somebody was beating him. He saw me and ran right at me, held onto my leg like a drownin' man. I picked him up and clear as day, he says, 'Help me, Grampa.' He calls me that sometimes, even though it puts his mother in a real bad state. Don't even know where he got the word; I sure didn't saddle him with it."

Wiz takes a deep breath. Sits back, chin in one hand, staring, then, "Where is he?"

"He's with somebody safe; that's a promise."

"Walter," I say when I can find my voice, "you let me think. . . . "

"I'm sorry, Annie," he says. "I know how scared you've been, but until I figured out what to do, I couldn't take any chances."

I'm so glad to know Frankie's okay, I don't know whether to feel relieved or betrayed. Bastard could have told me *any*time; he *has* to know I'd have never said a word.

"Walter," Wiz says, "this makes you . . . "

"A kidnapper," Walter says. "I know that. Knew it the minute I decided not to throw the little bugger back onto the Boots Whirligig. But I'm pushin' seventy, and it's not a young seventy—can barely sit on my hog more than half hour at a time. I could get three-to-five or life and there wouldn't be a lot of difference. Like I said, the boy's safe, where nobody will find him without me tellin' 'em."

"Jesus," Wiz says, almost to himself. "What am I

supposed to do here? I can't pretend I don't know this. I mean, we're talking criminal action."

Walter nods. "Your situation any more precarious than Frankie's?"

That stops Wiz cold.

"Listen," Walter says. "I been hearing about your outfit since way back, when I first met Annie's momma. I'll admit, I was never gonna get a clear picture from her, but Annie's a fan, much as she can be, and her version is just a cleaned-up version of Nancy's. I know you mean well, Wiz; I do. And I believe you'd *do* well if they'd let you. But man, you've got the occupation with the worst job satisfaction of any I can think of but maybe sewer taster."

"Walter, there are rules."

"Yes, there are, and you're handcuffed by them. I'm not. I'm not a religious man, Wiz; don't know God from no God from Christian God from Muslim God from Star Wars God. But I know this: there comes a time to account, if only to ourselves. If you'd seen that little boy's face when he asked me to save him . . . well . . . I was there an' I'm accountin'."

"So you'd go to jail."

"In a minute."

Wiz nods toward me. "And leave these people wondering . . . without their child."

"'Fraid so. I don't know a hell of a lot, but I do know in my world, the child comes first. You've never seen that little guy so calm as he is right now. Annie's going to find her way. Her mother's going to be in about the same pain, no matter; she's hardwired. Sheila's had about all the chances she has coming, and *nothing* has changed. I wouldn't be leaving anyone worse than I found them." Walter stands. "Think about it, Wiz. A woman gets into some domestic violence situation, runs, goes back, runs, goes back. You folks send her to some domestic violence therapy group that does it's absolute damnedest to convince her this guy isn't gonna change; yet you take a kid and keep puttin' him back and puttin' him back and puttin' him back. How's that make sense?"

Wiz strokes his chin, looks back and forth between me and Walter . . . for what seems like a *long* time. Finally he says, "Look, why don't the two of you go have some lunch and fight over how pissed Annie is about the fact that you didn't tell her." He frowns toward me. "I might have a plan, but I need to sit with it." He rises, extends his hand to Walter. "You have my word I won't do *anything* that you don't know about first."

I run around the table and hug Wiz.

꒳ ꒳ ꒳

"I just miss him," Marvin says. "It was no fun getting ahead of his bad habits, but watching him play and engaging in these way crazy conversations . . . it felt like I was helping him. I just miss him."

Marvin and I are out on a run. I've convinced him that thespian nerdiness doesn't necessarily preclude physical fitness, and he's agreed to give it a try. I don't expect instant results, but winning the Olympic marathon begins with the first step.

Marvin says, "You remember that line you said you read in a book once?"

"Which one?"

"Something like . . . 'If you want to see how something works . . . '"

I say, ". . . look at it broken."

"That's it. It's what it felt like playing with Frankie . . . like I was seeing a broken kid, and some things started making sense." He's giving it to me three words at a time, between gasps.

"Things like what?"

"Like how things work for people. I mean, look at what all's been said about Frankie; why he does that with his poop? Why does he engage in negative activity? It's about control, isn't that what you said?"

"I guess. That's what his therapists told my sister."

"Okay, so that's what he does when he feels out of control, which is most of the time. So you look at that and say, that's gotta be where control freaks come from. They're out of control so they get it any way they can. Right?"

"Marvin, it might be that you think too much. You're, like, too smart for your own good."

"Yeah, yeah, but do you follow?"

"I follow."

"Okay, so a little kid probably doesn't choose the right thing to get control of, because, well, he's a little kid. But take someone like my dad, who's gotta be in control of *everything*. You can't play a game without him pointing out your foolish mistakes. If he thinks I'm a little too much on the *sensitive* side, he has to tell me how tough I've gotta get. He's always talking to Mom about how some guy or woman at the office just up and quit. Think that might just be because he's as hard to work for as he is to live with?"

We're about a quarter mile from home because a *run* to Marvin is a much slower undertaking than it is for me. "I hope this is going further than *we're* going."

"It is; I wonder if my dad is broken. I mean, you almost never see him smile. He's like a radar machine, always scanning for what's out of control. I'll bet that's why he doesn't like Frankie very much. They're both fighting for control, but Frankie's more at a . . . like *primitive* level."

Marvin's right. When you're around Pop, you're always looking for the thing you might be doing wrong. Not *really* wrong, just wrong in his eyes. You're *never* not vigilant around him.

I say, "I don't know if I'd call him broken; I mean, he functions. You guys . . . *we're* relatively rich. He has a successful marriage with Momma."

"Maybe if you consider a marriage is successful because of its longevity," Marvin says, "but do you think my mom's happy? Can *he* have a successful marriage if she doesn't?"

"She's happy with you, Marvin. With *us*."

"That's motherhood," he says, "not marriage. Geez, can we walk a minute?" He's down to two big words per breath.

"You could run better if you'd quit talking."

"Why would I run without talking?" he says. "How boring is that?"

We switch to a relatively fast walk.

"So all this came from you watching Frankie play?"

"Sometimes it's hard to shut my mind off," he says. "But yeah, 'If you want to see how something works . . . '"

We walk in silence for a block or so, and just as I'm about to suggest that we break into a jog . . . "I'm worried if my dad is broken, I might be, too."

I've had that same thought about Nancy and me, especially when I look at Sheila. "I guess everyone with messed-up parents thinks that at one time or another."

"I heard my dad say if they find Frankie, he'll be banished from our home."

I *hate* that word. I say, "He thinks Frankie connects you guys to my family. He told me not letting Frankie come back is for my good as well as yours."

Marvin snorts. "My dad does *nothing* for somebody else's good. If they do find Frankie and Dad won't let him come back, I'm running away."

I laugh. "You better run faster than *this*."

"I just miss him." He chokes on it.

"I miss him, too," I say. We break into a slow jog, get another block, and I have to say it. "Can you keep a secret?"

"Yeah, I can keep a secret."

"I mean from *everyone*, but especially from your folks."

"For sure."

"They found Frankie."

He stops. "What? Alive?"

"Yup."

"Oh, God, where?"

"I don't know for sure, but somebody does."

"Do the cops know? Did anybody call 'em?"

"No. It's not a cop *thing*; at least I hope not. But serious, Marvin, you can't tell *anyone*. I told you because I know how it feels to wonder. Swear, buddy. *No*body hears this from you."

"I promise. I promise; I swear. God damn. But a time will come, right? Like when everyone knows?"

"Yeah, there'll be a time."

I really hope it's not a time when I'm visiting Walter in jail.

"Cell phones on the table," Wiz says, and I dig mine out of my pack. Walter removes his from his leather vest.

Wiz places his beside them. "Can't afford to see this conversation popping up on YouTube," he says, and leans his forearms on the conference room table. Wiz is one of those guys whose body is as strong as his mind—lean and sinewy with, like, *zero* body fat. He inspires trust. "I may have found a way out of this that works for everyone, Frankie especially."

Now Walter leans forward, too.

"If it doesn't work," Wiz says, "let's hope you and I get a cell together, Walter."

Walter grimaces. "I don't want you—"

Wiz holds up his hand. "All due respect, I didn't craft this little piece of trickery for what you want."

Walter turns his palms up.

"I ran this past my wife about two-thirty this morning. She's a pediatric nurse, so it was probably no fun losing the sleep, but she's been telling me for years to get into another line of work. This is the first time she thought maybe my career choice wasn't completely ill-thought-out."

"Seems like a righteous way to make a living to me," Walter says. He probably means relative to selling motorcycles, working intermittent night shifts at convenience stores, and doing odd jobs under the table.

"Yeah, well, righteous doesn't always get the job done. They pay you lower-middle-class wages, which is no big deal—no one figures to get rich off hurt kids—but then they put you in a strait jacket. They won't fund treatment programs they know would work because they cost too much, and the courts cater to parents' rights over kids' rights every time. We'll run a kid back and forth till they're exhausted just because the public defenders get some brand-new fresh-out-of-college, know-*nothing* therapist to say the parent is 'making progress.' You want to know what kind of progress Nancy Boots was making while she was trying to get Annie's sister back? She learned to sneak somebody else's pee into the bottle. She got smarter and smarter in parenting classes because she'd taken them so many times. Even Rance—he who doesn't leave a footprint—got infinite chances. We *knew*.

We had the best child developmentalist in the region, gave us cutting edge information on attachment. We should have taken *Nancy* into foster care and the kids with her; Rance if he was willing to go. If I remember right, that was Annie's idea. But that would be run by *experts*, and experts expect to be paid a decent wage. See, if Nancy messes up in that situation, the kids' needs are still covered. And if she can't make it, they *see* her not making it, instead of hearing that she can't, and having to listen to her lies about evil caseworkers during hour-long visits, and getting confused thinking there's something *they* could do; or should have done." He looks directly at me, sweat trickling down his temple. "What the hell," he says. "I'll get off my soapbox."

"But you're headed someplace with this," Walter says calmly. "To your idea about Frankie."

"Yes I am." He sits back. "Look, the only people who know Frankie's real situation, other than whoever's got him, are sitting here in this room. What if he reappears? Somebody brings him into social services, and I'm the one they bring him to. I get my expert to do the forensic interview, work with Officer Graham to let that interview stand for them as well as us; we provide the police a transcript. We place him, keep the placement confidential for his protection, put this bad boy to bed."

"How's that gonna be different," Walter asks. "Puts him right back where he was."

"Not if whoever's got him now is willing to keep him. He's got access to you there, and you're who he ran to. He can have contact with Nancy, through you, and Sheila if and when she shows back up."

"What if she gets clean?" I ask. "Won't they just give her one more chance?"

"There's that," Wiz says, "but I've known your sister since I started working with you and I knew *about* her before that. How many *true* clean and sober days do you think she's had in that time?"

I say, "Well, there was this one Wednesday . . . "

"Bad as her record is, we require a year. She blows it once, we terminate. At the same time, we do what Kennedy and the Russians called 'back-door negotiations' where on her good days she gets to see him."

"God," I say. "Sometimes I don't even know if she wants to."

"This plan gives us our best chance of finding out."

Walter's fingers drum on the table. "And if this doesn't work? If somebody finds you out?"

"I take the heat," Wiz says. "All of it. Your name never comes up."

"You could go to jail. Prison."

"I could," Wiz says. "That's the part that excites my wife."

"I'm serious."

"Seriously, I *could* go to prison, but there's a far better chance I'd lose my job and be on probation. My kids are grown, my wife makes good money, I could get a job doing something useful. Plus, my lifestyle's so damn tame I don't break probation *now*, and I'm not on it."

"Lot of ways this could go bad," Walter says. "I don't like puttin' you in this position."

"Hell with it, Walter. I should thank you. I'm tired of pretending to help."

And like that. We have a plan.

CHAPTER
THIRTEEN

"Annie," Pop says. "I need to apologize to you."

I can tell by the tone, this isn't a real apology.

"We've let this silly 'losers bracket' thing play out, even watched you sabotage your scholarship chances wasting time on sports you had no business playing. And look what it came to."

Through barely un-gritted teeth, "What did it come to?"

"Ultimately, to the fiasco at the swim meet," he says. "To Frankie's disappearance."

I sit forward. "It's *my* fault Frankie's gone?"

"I didn't say that. But even you have to admit—"

I throw up my hands. "Just tell me the rules, Pop." I can't

stand to hear the same old thing over and over.

"Fine. No more Boots," he says. "No more sitting in the stands with them between games, no more sneaking off to coffee or shopping. No more *chance* meetings. If you run into Nancy or Sheila, you nod and walk on. I guess I should say the same about Rance, but he's no threat to anything. I wouldn't recognize the guy if I saw him on the street."

I calm the feeling in my stomach. "If I run into Nancy on the street, like *really* by coincidence, I don't walk past without saying something. I can't make a promise like that."

Momma says, "Honey, she has a point."

Pop shoots a *don't defy me* glare, then looks away. "Very well—one sentence of acknowledgement then; that's it. Now, do we agree, or do I need to add consequences?"

And people wonder why kids lie.

I say, "I understand."

"Good. Why don't you spend the rest of the day in your room, thinking it over. Let's be sure we don't have this conversation again."

The one thing he's said that I agree with.

Momma is massaging her temples.

I'm nervous about Frankie's reappearance. It's like the good guys in all those cop shows say; when you set out to commit the perfect crime, there are a hundred things to consider and you're lucky if you think of seven. DNA trails and security cameras and smart phones and dumb people saying the wrong thing at the wrong time can trip you up at any point. I'm not part of the planning of any of this, but I could fit into that last category if the stars line up right. Plus, I'm carrying some anxiety around because, as much as she pisses me off, I worry about my sister. She can come off mean as a snake, but when she goes *down,* like to depression, anything could happen. Plus, I don't want Walter to go to jail or Wiz to lose his job, or Frankie to end up on the foster care merry-go-round. And I *really* worry that it could all end up being because of me. Much as I hate the way Pop puts it, if I hadn't had to have it both ways with my two families, hadn't been the catalyst for bringing Frankie into the Howards' lives, this would never have gotten so complicated. But I swear, when I look back remembering who I was as that little kid trying to figure out how to get back to a mother who couldn't take care of me, a sister I banged heads with *hourly,* and a ghost dad, I can't see what I could have done differently. The *draw* alone has always felt like what I imagine addiction to be. When anxiety reaches a certain level, you'll do *anything* to bring it down.

I can't mess up my little part.

So I'm dutifully in my room, helping keep the peace in

the Howard household, when my cell pings.

Walter: Meet for coffee?

Me: Sure. Give me an extra half hour. Kinda grounded. Will be on my bike.

Walter: Never mind. We'll do it another time. Don't get in trouble.

Me: Wouldn't feel right without trouble. Leaving now. See you there.

So much for keeping the peace.

Walter's buying, so this must be serious.

He says, "We've got a small problem. Might need your help."

"Sure, Walter."

"I didn't want you involved in this. . . . "

"Hey, I'm, like, the *author* of it."

"The *calm* I said Frankie was experiencin' is starting to crack. He loves seeing me every day, but it's not enough; he needs more familiar faces."

"Think I should go see him? I can do that, soon as I smooth things over with Pop." The *only* way I smooth things over with Pop is to eat huge helpings of humble pie.

"That would be good," he says, "but he's achin' for his momma. Even if he can't live with her, I think he needs to see that she's okay . . . have a visit and let her explain things—under supervision, a'course"

"Who knows where *she* might be?"

"I went back and checked her old place on the off chance, but it was rented out."

"So what do we do?"

"We need to have things lined up when Frankie reappears for real. If anybody knows her whereabouts, it'd be that Yvonne girl. I tracked her down, but she wouldn't let me past the crack in the door she told me to go to hell through."

I laugh. "That's Yvonne. She probably sees you through the same eyes as Sheila."

"Kinda what I thought," he says. "'Worthless ancient biker' isn't a term you hear twice by coincidence."

"So what can I do?"

"Go see her; feel her out for what she knows. If she could lead us to Sheila, maybe we can figure something out—get to her before Wiz takes Frankie public an' gets her all pissed off. Got her address right here." He hands me a folded piece of paper.

"Yvonne! Come on! Open up! I know you're in there. I saw you through the window when I was coming up the steps." I yell it through the door.

I came straight from coffee with Walter; I need to hurry. When Pop finds out I didn't honor his demand that I spend the rest of the day in my room, he may chain me to the wall.

"Go away! I don't know where she is!"

"That's not why I'm here! C'mon, open up!"

I wait long enough that I think she's blowing me off, but as I'm starting down the apartment house steps to run around back, the door opens. "What?"

"Can I come in?"

"What do you want?"

"Let me in and I'll tell you."

We stare at each other through the crack for a moment, then she steps back, for which I thank her.

Yvonne has always looked "unfortunate" to me. She's a big woman, about Sheila's height but without the muscled structure that is a Boots trademark. If she didn't look so incredibly sad she might be pretty. I don't know much about her, really; just that she's hung around Sheila the last few years and is incredibly loyal. She must have a high tolerance for being treated like shit, because when Sheila's not feeling good, which is about a hundred percent of the time, she's no fun.

I ask if it's okay for me to sit and she shrugs, so I do.

"I know you said you don't know where my sister is, but

you've got a better chance of hearing from her than anyone," I say.

"What makes you think that? Seems like she'd call her boyfriend."

"She has a boyfriend?"

She shrugs. "Doesn't she always have a boyfriend?"

"I guess. Sounds like you don't like that much."

"They're all assholes."

"Yeah," I say, "she's a magnet for bad guys."

Yvonne looks away.

"Listen, if she does get in touch, tell her to call me. My old caseworker says until they discover otherwise, they're assuming Frankie will turn up, so they're setting up a plan."

"What kind of plan?"

"Depending on what she's willing to do, a plan with the best chance of her not losing contact with him. Like, significant contact."

Yvonne just stares at me.

"That is, if she even wants it. Truth, Yvonne, I'm not even sure."

She drops her face to her hands. "I miss him so much. I'm the one that took care of him; I mean, when she wasn't pawning him off on you guys. The little guy would do *anything* just to get a pat on the head from her, but she just cursed him and said how he'd ruined her life. If she'd have moved in with me, I could have kept him safe. I wanted her . . . " and she trails off.

"You're really in love with her."

"And I treated her good," she says finally. "Not like all those . . . those assholes. I treated them both like . . . " and her entire body heaves.

"Like a mom, huh?"

She lets out a weak cry.

"Look, Yvonne, you don't know me very well; mostly you've just seen me as Sheila's bitchy little sister. But for the first time in the history of caseworkers *ever*, I think they're going to surround Frankie with something like a family if they find him. Sheila could be part of it, and if she were, you could be, too." I stand up. "So . . . if she calls."

Yvonne walks me to the door, where she grips my wrist. "Annie, I don't know whether you know it or not, but right before all this happened there was a complaint called into social services."

"I know."

"It was me," she says, "and you *do* know there's almost no chance he's alive. This is my fault." She looks truly anguished.

I take her other hand. "Listen to me. I have *really* good reason to think he is. Be ready."

"You have a minute?" Marvin peeks in my room, to where I have been once again banished. I am on a *short* leash.

"I've got way longer than that."

"Maybe not," Marvin says, and a closer look reveals red eyes.

"What?"

"Dad is talking about expelling you. He's thinking about calling children's services in the morning to say he can't handle you."

"He'll get over it. You know how he is."

Marvin says, "I hate him."

"C'mon, Marvin. He's your dad."

"All the more reason to hate him," Marvin says. "It would be different if just some bad guy was doing this. He sounds like he means it this time."

I'm looking calm for Marvin's sake, but adrenaline runs through me like a river. I didn't think it would go this far. "You know, Marvin, he has a point. The only reason he's 'handled' me this long is I let him."

"I get it; you're a pain in the patoot; big news. But where would you go?"

"I'm seventeen. Wiz could help me get emancipated. I'll bet Leah could talk her parents into taking me in till the end of the school year. Leah could talk anyone into anything. After that, I'm gone anyway."

"I wish my mom would divorce him."

"Your mother is *not* going to divorce your dad. Certainly not because of *me*."

"Well, she should. Everything always has to be his way. I might run away." His eyes narrow. "If you go, I go."

"Look, maybe Pop's just mad. Maybe he'll get over it. If he decides to put me out for real, he'll drag me into the den to tell me why fifteen times. I'll have a chance to talk him out of it."

"You're right. He is angry. If you'd let me tell him about Frankie's situation—"

"No! Marvin, everything with Frankie has to work just right."

"But he couldn't stay angry if he knows it's all about Frankie."

"Look, you and I, like, care a lot more about Frankie than Pop does; you have to know that. He's been cool about taking him, but if it hadn't been for Momma, things would be real different. So, whatever Wiz comes up with has to be our truth, okay? Just for now."

"This is unjust."

"Promise me."

He sets his jaw.

"Marvin, I'll kill you if you tell. And I'll leave anyway."

Surface tension keeps a single tear from falling. "I know. I'm not going to tell; I promised. I just don't want you to leave. You're the only person I really talk to."

"*And*, he'd turn all that crap onto you."

He leans back and kind of laughs. "There's that." He laughs harder. "Annie, if you abandon me I'll be left in the driveway shooting hoops with that . . . that . . . "

"Yeah," I say, "who *wouldn't* want somebody between them and Pop. Look, if he boots me, you can meet up with me like I do with Nancy, and really piss him off."

A hard knock. "Annie!"

"Yeah, Pop."

"Is Marvin in there?"

Marvin's head snaps up. I put my finger to my lips and point to my bathroom. He silently moves there under cover of my coughing fit. "No."

"Well, if he wants in you tell him you're grounded. From all conversation. I don't want him tainted with all this. We have serious business to discuss."

"I'll tell him," I say, staring at the door between two raised middle fingers.

Incoming text:

Walter: You watching the TV?

Me: No

Walter: Turn it on. Channel 6.

I hit the remote, click on channel 6, and there's Frankie—or a picture of him—followed by a live shot of Wiz standing on the steps in front of his office building answering questions. The ticker at the bottom of the screen says, "Frankie Boots, once believed kidnapped, found alive and unharmed."

Wiz fields questions, calm as can be, from the three network affiliates, public TV, the *Spokesman-Review*, and the *Inlander*. He received a text telling him to go immediately to the lobby, where he discovered Frankie sitting in a chair. No, the text wasn't traceable; it came from a burner cell phone. Yes, the police have been notified, and later this afternoon Officer Graham and Wiz will hold another news conference. Frankie was calm; seems healthy, with no visible marks and no noticeable trauma. No, Wiz will not reveal Frankie's whereabouts, will only say he's in temporary placement while the department figures out the next move. The mother has not been notified because her whereabouts are unknown; finding her is a high priority. The department has no comment as to Frankie's placement should the mother be found and will not comment on rumors there was a pending CPS complaint. And on and on.

I burst out of my room to get ahead of the curve, which gives Marvin a chance to slip out behind me. "Turn on the TV!"

Pop says, "I thought I told you—"

"They found Frankie! Turn on the TV! Channel six!"

Pop punches the remote in time to see old footage of Sheila pleading for his return.

"I'll be damned," Pop says. "How in the world . . . "

I stare at the screen and give him the short version of what I just saw in my bedroom.

The news dazed Pop to the extent that he put our war on hold. But just when I think I can coast under his radar a while longer, we end up in the den.

"Annie, do you have any idea why I've set up this meeting?"

God, who "sets up" a meeting in their own family? I glance around the den; déjà vu. The two overstuffed chairs sit face-to-face, Pop in one, the other waiting to be graced with *my* butt. I say, "Yes."

"Tell me."

"No."

Pop looks like I elbowed him, like, in the groin. "Excuse me?"

"No. You called me in here. Say it." I see by the look on his face that Marvin or no Marvin, I can't save this.

"Young lady, I'm pretty tired of your impudence."

"I'm pretty tired of being imprisoned in my room . . . and I haven't been impudent. I've been sneaky and I've been disobedient, but when it comes to impudence, I am not guilty."

"Fine. Sneaky and disobedient it is. Before this evening is over, we're going to take care of that."

"Bet we don't," I say as I decide to get ahead of the curve. "You 'called this meeting' to throw me out of your house."

"What makes you think that?"

"You know. Rumors. Thin walls. Heat duct between Marvin's room and yours."

"What? Has Marvin . . . "

"Marvin doesn't know I go in there," I say. "File that under 'Annie's Sneakiness.'"

He grits his teeth. I hope he's thinking of all the things Marvin may have heard through that heat duct. But he does what he does best, which is to stay *on task*. "Actually, I've called you in to help you with some tough choices."

"Which are . . . "

"Until this last year, we found solutions to our differences, would you agree? You followed general rules, didn't just directly disobey my orders."

"Yeah, if you don't count the Boots thing. But we didn't find solutions. You found solutions and I lied and agreed with you."

"Well, your perspective is what it is, but while I didn't call you in here to 'throw you out of my house,' as you put it, I am telling you that until you graduate, there'll be no more meeting up with . . . what can I call it . . . your history. Not at games, not at these 'chance' meetings. Nothing. No contact."

"Pop, what's changed? We had this conversation two weeks ago. I told you, I am not ignoring them on the street."

"Then you do what you need to do to not be on the street when they are. What's changed is that *immediately* after that last conversation, you went right to your room and out the window. I've thought about it; I put you right back in there, but there's no guarantee you'll stay."

"I didn't go out the window. I went out the front door. You were in here congratulating yourself on another fine job of putting your foot on my neck."

"Well, Annie, we're down to it. My foot is on your neck. Your contact with those people, other than what needs to happen with Frankie, is finished."

This is crazy. My fuse isn't even lit. "And if it isn't . . . "

"*Then* I'm afraid you'll have to find another place to finish out the year."

I smile. "You figured a way to throw me out without throwing me out. I'll bet you're a really good businessman."

If this were one of those old-time cartoons, Pop would turn bright red and his head would explode. "That's enough!"

He still hasn't figured out that I don't care. My head is with Walter and Wiz—and Frankie—and hopefully Sheila and maybe even Nancy. "Did Momma have anything to say about this?" I ask.

"This has nothing to do with her. This is my decision."

"You know about the Nineteenth Amendment, right?"

"What?"

"Women's right to vote."

"You just can't stop with the smart mouth, can you? Annie, what's happened to you? Do you realize what's at stake?"

I nod very slowly. "My self-respect. My happiness."

"Your college education," he says. "As it stands, I'm on the hook for that."

I have *never* felt this calm in this kind of storm. "Well, I'm taking you off. You know what makes this so easy?"

He glares. In this instant it is *so* clear how Pop's entire self-image depends on his capacity to be the boss.

"That you think you're putting my future on the line. That's a hammer no kid should live under."

The muscle in his jaw turns into a marble.

"So, I'll get my stuff." I lean forward. "And by the way, poor people go to college all the time. It's not easy, but if they really want to, they go."

I rise to leave, and am startled to see Momma just on the other side of the paned glass door. So she was in on this, too. *That* breaks my heart.

I open the door to slide past her. "Stay right where you are, baby."

Pop starts to get up.

"You stay where you are, too, *baby.*"

"Jane, this has nothing to do with you. This is me holding Annie responsible for her own future."

Momma actually picks up a book from the nearest shelf and hurls it right at his head. "You arrogant son-of-a-bitch!" she yells. "What do you mean it has nothing to do with me? This is *my* house and *my* daughter and if someone's leaving, it's you."

Pop is unflappable. "Jane, I know you mean well . . . "

And Momma hurls another book.

"Stop that!"

"Then shut your mouth!"

"You need to understand, this is a pivotal time in Annie's . . . " and he's ducking another book. The first two were paperback. This one's a John Irving hardback.

"This is a pivotal time in *your marriage*," Momma says in a low voice, reaching for another book. "A time in which the next two words out of your mouth better be 'Yes, ma'am.' And the three after that better be 'I'm sorry, Annie.'"

Pop is a highly regarded business man in this town and he *really* doesn't like being pushed around, and he remains true to his jock philosophy that the best defense is a powerful offense. "Jane, you're about to get into territory that's very hard to retreat from."

"It's *impossible* to retreat from," Momma says, "and you will by God not see me take one step backward. I just gave you two short, easily learnable lines that could have led to a two percent chance of saving your marriage and you blew them. By the end of this day, one of us is going to be out of this house."

The only sound is that of her retreating footsteps.

Pop is stunned, but only for a moment before going after her. He says, "Now look what you've done," as he passes me.

I'm putting things into my duffel when I hear the knock.

"Hey, Marvin."

"Somebody dropped a bomb right into the middle of my family."

"Sorry, pal. It was me."

"It was Mom," he says.

"I'm sorry anyway."

"I'm not," Marvin says. "I was hating the idea of growing up, thinking I'd have to act like my dad to succeed."

"You knew you wouldn't though, right?"

He points at my heart. "Whoever said you were nothing but a jock."

I point back. "Better not have been you. What's going on out there?"

He smiles. "Dad's at the bedroom door. He was hollering, now he's pleading. I was using their bathroom when she locked him out. When I came out, she was logging onto the bank website.

"What do you think will happen?"

He shrugs. "Whatever it is, my life will be better. If they break up, you and I live with Mom here or wherever she goes, and all of a sudden he has to be nice to me because I become a bargaining chip. If they stay together, Mom doesn't let him expel you and he goes on living vicariously through your athletic exploits—though he won't enjoy it as much—and treating me like the gay son he never wanted."

I laugh. "You have to start bringing home a girlfriend."

He sticks out his lower lip and snorts. "I don't care if my

189}

dad thinks I'm gay. I don't care if anyone thinks I'm gay. Some of the nicest guys I know are gay, and *all* of the assholes I know are straight."

"Remember your logic course. Just because all assholes are straight, not all straight guys are assholes."

"*Hell* yeah. *I'm* cool, for one. Not so much my dad."

"You're not giving him much slack."

"He reeled it all in," Marvin says, "when he tried to get rid of you."

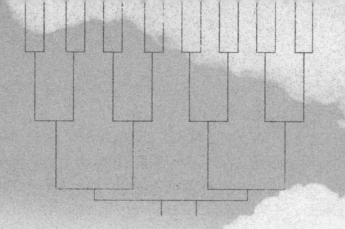

CHAPTER
FOURTEEN

"**A**ppreciate the ride," Walter says as Leah pulls in front of his place. We treated him to dinner and a showing at the Magic Lantern of a documentary on Bill Russell, the legendary center for the Boston Celtics of the late fifties and all of the sixties.

"Any time," Leah says. "You know the good places." Who'd have thought Walter was a basketball fan.

"Put it on my gravestone," he says, opening the door. "And the next time you all have a 'hero' talk at your book club, add Mr. Russell to the mix. The man *never* backed down. You all can have your Jordans an' LeBrons and Kobes. Give me the old-timers."

"Big surprise you're an old-timer's fan," Leah says. "What are you, like a hundred and ten?"

Walter is right about Bill Russell. According to this documentary, the guy stood for justice as much or more than any athlete of his century. The documentary inspired me; I'm going to see if I can get the group to read *Second Wind*. If I have trouble, Leah will push it through. I mean, Bill Russell started out in the NBA when the unwritten rule was that you kept more white guys on the court than black; when northern teams traveled to the south only to discover they needed two sets of team accommodations. Russell, arguably the best player in the world, threatened to sit out, or leave, whenever and wherever equality wasn't embraced. Leah is a black swimmer, and while she doesn't face *that* kind of discrimination, she's aware there have been two—count 'em, *two*—American black Olympic gold medalists, and she knows plenty of history to understand why. When the starter gun fires, every other swimmer in the race sees second place as a win.

We watch Walter saunter up his walk, then Leah takes me home, where things have remained in flux. No one actually left after the big fight, but it's been chilly around here for the past week and a half. I still have a room and a place at the dinner table, but Pop doesn't speak to me unless he has to, and his wife and son are barely speaking to him. Momma and Pop are in counseling, but I'd hate to be the therapist. In the late night, I've heard bellowed versions of " . . . all I've done for that girl!" accompanied by " . . . undermining my authority," followed by a door slamming and the sound of footsteps fading toward the living room. I have a feeling Pop is going to get tired of sleeping on the couch. The one word I hear over and over from Momma is "narcissist," which until recently I'd never even heard. I guess the best definition is, "It's all about me; like, *all* about me." I mean, how else can you explain the fact that he doesn't understand what a big deal finding Frankie was. The minute he heard he was safe, all he wanted was to make sure nobody related to Frankie ever got back into our lives.

When I asked Momma if things would be better if I found a place, she said, "Things will get better when Jack gets his head out of his ass, and he best speed it up. You just hang tough, sweetie."

I think Pop believes that if he continues with the silent treatment, I'll come around with a big apology, and I *have* apologized for escaping to Revel right after he grounded me to my room, but I can't apologize for my life; if I'm going to make that one, my apology needs to be to *me*. My draw to my mother, and to a lesser extent, to Sheila and even Rance, was a real thing. Maybe it wasn't good for me, but it was— and *is*—real. I've told myself a million lies, *way* more than I've told Pop—how that need wasn't really important and how stupid I am for even having it and how I'm tough enough to live this double life.

And it's worn me out. It's hard enough remembering what lie you last told so you don't rat yourself out with the next one, but it's hard-times-ten making yourself believe that what you *want* to be true *is* true when it is so clearly not.

Marvin is still rooting for the crack in the family fabric to split wide open. "Every other weekend with him would be just about right," he says.

We're at a back booth in Morty's—Wiz, Walter, and me—having early—as in before school—breakfast. "Official business," Wiz said when we ordered. "Eat up. Could be our last meal on the state's dime."

I say, "Are you in trouble?"

"Let's just say it's possible I could have thought this out better," he says, smiling. "Officer Graham knows Frankie's reappearance isn't legit, but he's playing 'don't ask, don't tell.' I'm supposed to talk with the regional supervisor at work later. We came up through the system together and she thinks a lot like I do, but this won't pass the smell test for her. Jeff

Humphries from the paper is hounding her for answers I won't give him. That guy can smell a rat."

"What are you telling him?" Walter asks.

"Stonewalling with my original story: Got a text from an unknown party, went downstairs, found Frankie in the lobby, tried to locate his absent mother, and when we couldn't, placed him in receiving care." Wiz laughs. "Way too pat for Humphries."

"Bet he gets tired of hearing that," I say.

Wiz nods. "We've done a faster-than-ever home study, got an emergency license. The caseworker is assigned, and we're setting up therapy. This would be a good time for a local serial killer or a hotel fire to give Humphries something else to do."

Walter runs his face over his hand. "I hate to throw in a wrinkle. . . . "

"There are gonna be a few," Wiz says. "Sooner the better."

"This is a big one. I went out to the Crawford's yesterday; checking up and keeping contact with the little bugger and . . . it looks like they're not gonna be able to keep him."

Wiz eyes close. "Shhhhhhh . . . What happened?"

"Economic reality," Walter says. "They've been juggling finances to keep their mortgage paid up, and it finally caught up with them. Looks like they're gonna lose the place. Where they're gonna land is . . . unknown."

Wiz closes his eyes and sighs. "I best go get him, then," he says. "Sooner the better. You wanna go with me, Walter? He's going to need a familiar face."

I say, "I can go, too."

"You've got school."

"I'll call the attendance office in my sick voice, tell them I'll bring a note in the morning."

"Why not?" Wiz says. "When this all falls apart, contributing to your truancy will be the lesser charge they can drop."

The waiter brings our breakfast and we dig in. After a bit, Wiz puts his fork down. "Where in the world are we going to put him?"

We drive in a state car several miles north of Spokane to a farm outside Colbert. Walter has called ahead, and a man whose age looks to be somewhere between Wiz and Walter meets us in the driveway. He's apologizing as we get out of the car.

"No sweat, Orland," Walter says. "Couldn'ta seen this coming, right?"

"Wish that were true," Orland says. "I've been robbing Peter to pay Paul for too long, hoping I could keep it going, but no can do. Julia's pretty embarrassed."

Wiz holds up his *halt!* hand. "It's okay, Orland; you've got your hands full, and you bought us time." He introduces me, and Orland invites us in.

"Annie!" Frankie shoots across the kitchen in an attempt to bowl me over.

"Hey, bud! I haven't seen you for*ever!*"

"I gots to move again," Frankie says. "Do I get to go with you? To Marvin's house?"

I glance at Wiz. "You'll get to see Marvin sometime soon," I say, "but we're not going to his house right yet."

"Is my mom still gone?"

"We're lookin' for her," Wiz says. "Got a feeling . . . " and he lets it trail off. He learned a long time ago not to say wishes out loud to little kids.

Walter drifts into the living room, and I hear muffled voices. In a minute or two he appears in the doorway and motions to me. "The missus wants to meet you."

Julia Crawford is dressed in an army T-shirt and camo pants—real government issue. Julia must have been a soldier. She shakes my hand and smiles kind of sheepishly. "I'm *so* sorry. . . . " She nods toward the doorway, toward Frankie's nonstop chatter. "He talks about you all the time," she says. "Are you going to be there for him?"

"Yes, ma'am."

"And if you have any influence over that sister of yours . . . "

I laugh. "Well, I make her pretty mad, if that counts."

"See if you can make her mad enough to be real in his life. I can see"—and she nods at Walter and points toward the kitchen—"there are a lot of people who love this little troublemaker, but this boy needs his mother. Even if she can't take care of him—he needs her somehow."

I feel the pang. "*Somehow* is about how he'll get her, if at all. I'll see if I can make her mad enough to act different."

Julia pats my hand. "All right then. You all clear the road for Frankie. Little guy's gonna need a wide one."

My *gut* tells me I should be angry, thinking of this one more loss, but the Crawfords did us a solid, as they say—I mean, they could wind up as accessories, right?

"Isn't it illegal in this state to talk on your cell while driving?" I ask. Wiz has two wheels in the gravel on the edge of the road as he tries to dial and drive.

"Add it to the charges," he says, and corrects back onto the pavement. "Aiding and abetting a kidnapper, lying to the police, ignoring my superiors, and talking on a cell phone while driving. Should get two life sentences at least." He finishes punching in the numbers. Geez, doesn't he know about Contacts? Or Siri?

This side of the conversation:

"Hey, honey . . . Yeah, I'm driving but I've got the earphone in (liar). . . . Listen, remember how you said our life was getting boring—kids gone, go to work, come home, have a drink and dinner, watch TV, go to bed, repeat? . . . Well, I think I have an idea how to break some of those boring habits. . . . No, I want it to be a surprise. . . . No, just promise you'll give it a try, or at least hear me out. . . . Hey, have I ever disappointed you? . . . Okay, there was that . . . yeah, and that. . . . Okay, okay, but this will be an adventure. . . . Yeah, if it doesn't work out, we can get divorced. . . . Love you, too, bye."

He looks to us. "She has a real sense of humor."

I say, "Does that mean Frankie's going where I think he's going?"

"It does if you think he's going to my place," Wiz says. "We've had our foster license for thirty years, took in a few over the years. I figure the safest way to keep Frankie from ratting us all out is to give him a place to rat where no one can hear."

"He's a load, Wiz," I say. "You remember what he *does,* right?"

"Everybody in the department knows what he does. In my division 'Frankie Boots' is a verb. But my wife was a child therapist before she got her nursing license; she's got some tricks up her sleeve. Plus, I live on the back road to Coeur d' Alene, so he'll still be out of sight. Won't tell the press where he is because of confidentiality. The farther we get away from the original event, the better our chance of it all dying down."

"So what's the next problem needs solved?" Walter asks.

"Permanent placement," Wiz says. "My wife can take time off, but that won't last forever. I thought we'd have no trouble expanding the Howards' license, since Annie's there and they're familiar with Frankie, but they seem resistant. Annie, do you know anything about that?"

"I know a lot about that." I give him the short version of the battle on the home front.

"Well, we gotta work this one problem at a time," Wiz says. "The principal at Frankie's school is on board, so nobody there will be talking to the press, but in the Twitter and Facebook world, rumors fly. Eventually we'll have to answer some."

"It's like football," Walter says. "Got your play set; there's a way it's supposed to unfold. Then the ball gets hiked."

Wiz laughs and nods. "It is very much like football."

"But touchdowns do get scored," Walter says.

"Unfortunately, by both sides," Wiz says, and grips Walter's shoulder. "I just want you to know that whatever happens, you won't be touched. If things go too far south, I'll fall on the sword. It's starting to look like time for that second career anyway."

I say, "Wiz. Frankie's *my* relative. Like I said before, I'm the only person here who's technically a juvenile, and I could think of a good story. Probably a *great* story."

"Not happenin'," Wiz says. "I work for child *protection*."

Walter says, "Let's all take a breath. No need to start solving problems that might never occur."

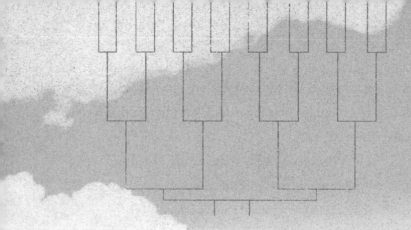

CHAPTER
FIFTEEN

"**A**ll my plans are shot to shit," Sheila says from the backseat of Leah's car. She texted me three days ago to pick her up at the bus station—"*an' by god you better not tell anybody I'm coming*"—so she's already mad that we're in Leah's car, even though I told her my access to transportation is pretty much consigned to my bike since the onset of the Howard's civil war. I took a chance and, with Walter's blessing, had brought Leah up to speed on the whole enterprise.

"Somethin's fishy," Sheila says.

Leah asks what she means.

"You just drive," Sheila says. "Ain't none of your business."

Leah shrugs. "Fine. All I care about is your son."

So *I* ask Sheila what she means.

"Kid disappears into thin air. I go beggin' on TV for whatever scumbag took him to bring him back. Nothin' happens. I give up an' go off 'cause I'm startin' to hear all this negative shit about myself, like how I didn't watch my kid . . . and abra-fuckin'-cadabra, he shows up. At social services, for chrissake, right where they were fixin' to take him away from me in the first place. He ain't harmed, nobody done nothin' nasty to him? Then somebody figures out Yvonne might know where I am an' next thing I'm hearing from you. Like I said, somethin's fishy."

I say, "What do you think it is?" Contradicting her would only etch her belief deeper in stone.

"Hell if I know," she says, "but when I find out, heads are gonna roll. An' I'll betcha some of them work for the state, an' if I find out some social worker had something to do with it . . . "

"C'mon, Sheila, you sure that's where you wanna focus? Are you gonna spend all your energy getting even? Or are you gonna do what it takes to do right by Frankie? Seems like right now a social worker would be your best friend. And *I'm* the one who figured Yvonne might know."

"Ain't no social worker *ever* been my best friend. They were gonna take him."

I say "They weren't going to take him until he disappeared, Sheila. Somebody saw his arm and you were about to get a visit, but if he's not bleeding out, they don't pull him. Just because there was a CPS report doesn't mean a kid gets automatically yanked. However, take those bruises along with him disappearing from under your nose . . . "

"Fuck you."

Leah grips the wheel. "*That's* where Frankie learned to talk like that."

"Fuck you, too," she says again. "*Somebody's* gonna lose their job."

Leah glances into the rearview mirror. "Somebody's gonna lose their kid."

Sheila whacks the back of my head. "Where'd you find *this* bitch?"

I say, "Pulled her out of the deep end."

Sheila sits back hard in the seat. Folds her arms.

Leah says. "Where to?"

Silent contempt covers Sheila's face.

"Come on, Sheila," I say. "We can't just drive around all afternoon. Your old place is rented out. You want to go to Nancy's?"

It takes a second but she finally says, "Yeah. Nancy's."

That's a reunion I'm going to be happy to miss.

"I hate that bitch." Sheila's once again in the backseat.

I say, "Good thing we stayed around."

"Yvonne's?" Leah says.

Sheila grunts.

We weren't at Nancy's five minutes before Nancy accused Sheila of abandoning Frankie after she "sucked up all the damn TV sympathy" and Sheila was accusing Nancy of . . . well pretty much everything up to and including global terrorism. Their only point of agreement was the future firebombing of social and health services. And after all that, when Sheila said she was going to Yvonne's, Nancy said she could stay.

Now in the car, Sheila says, "Minute she heard I was going to Yvonne's, all of a sudden she changes her tune."

I laugh. "Nancy thinks Yvonne is turning you away from acceptable Nancy Boots behavior."

"Ma's a fuckin' bigot."

I *refuse* to explain the concept of irony. "Sheila," I say, "you gotta quit doing dumb things. You gotta get clean, get a place, keep all the Butches in your life away from Frankie till he's eighteen."

No answer. I turn to see tears rolling down her cheeks.

"I'm not gonna get another chance with Frankie," she says. "I got nobody." She's quiet another minute, then, "I never done right by Frankie 'cause I never even knew if I wanted 'im. Only when they said they was gonna take him. That's when. And I don't know if I love him or I just didn't want somebody takin' one more damn thing from me."

It *kills* me when my sister's shell cracks. It's so much easier to do battle with a hard-ass. "Look," I say. "I know you've always hated me, and I've always hated you. But you had the right and I didn't. I got put someplace where they took care of me. And they took me back when things fell apart. You went to foster homes where people who should have never have gotten their hands on you did. You took way more shit from Nancy because you were first; she's always been meaner to you."

"Just shut up, Annie," she says.

"No. When this is all done you're going to hate my guts again, and that will make me hate you right back. So I'm getting it said. You've got one shot, which means Frankie has one shot. Remember, *you're* the one who said neither of us could afford to turn into Nancy."

She drops her head and the tears fall straight to the floor. "I *am* fuckin' Nancy."

Leah pulls to the curb and turns around in her seat. "Not yet."

"Leave me alone. You don't know me."

"Actually," Leah says, "I'm starting to."

"Well," Wiz says, "looks like my long career pretending to protect children is drawing to a close."

We're gathered around a wooden table in a conference room at children's services; me, Wiz, Walter, and Momma, who Wiz is still hoping will step up for permanent placement. We're a day past the return of Sheila.

I say, "What happened?"

"Got ratted out."

"By who?"

Wiz smiles. "Me."

"Does this fall into the category of 'sabotaging behavior'?" I ask, calling up a term Wiz used on me throughout my grade school years.

"I'm gratified," he says, "that the entirety of my wisdom wasn't flushed down the toilet with my job."

"Does it?" I wait.

"Willful sabotage," he says, and sits back. "You know how they say most criminals are caught because they don't think of half the things they need to think of before they commit the crime?"

Great minds think alike. "Can't tell you how many times I heard that when I was little, when Nancy was still with Rance."

"I'm supposed to be smarter than Rance," Wiz says.

"I guess if I take them up on the five free therapy sessions included in my retirement package, I'll discover I knew all along where this was going."

"What happened, Wiz?" Momma says.

"Humphries, the *Review* reporter, did his job. Officer Graham was more than willing to let it die, but Humphries kept pumping in the oxygen."

Walter says, "You being charged? Hell, man, let me take the hit for this. It was my doing."

Wiz shakes his head. "Naw, this story is a snake eating its tail. No way I can extract myself from it completely, so there's no reason for both of us to go down. I told RoyAnne, my supe, the whole story, without using your name, of course, and she's sympathetic, but she had to do something; rumors were flying around the department like drones. If Sheila is going to have a chance to pull it together, we can't let the public know definitively that Frankie was about to be removed. None of their business anyway, but you know what social media would look like. So I resign, RoyAnne says mistakes were made but the person who made them is no longer with us; can't discuss any further because of confidentiality. If Sheila doesn't get oral diarrhea, there's no one else for Humphries to talk to. We'll weather him and the TV folks for a few weeks and all will be well."

"Except you are out of a job," Walter says.

"Best part of it," Wiz says. "I've got retirement built up, some in savings. Wife works, and *she's* wanted me out of this business since before I got into it. Gives me enough cushion to get into a fast-track master's program in education and go where I can do some real good."

Momma says, "You wouldn't say all this just to make us all feel better, would you Wiz?"

"I would," he says, "but I'm not."

Momma says, "Mmm-hmm."

"Margie Waters has been assigned the case. Her fingerprints aren't anywhere on it. If we can get Frankie into foster-adopt . . . well, that's the best we can do. Sheila gets it together, she gets her shot. If not, he'll be somewhere permanent." He turns to Momma. "Which I was fantasizing would be your place."

"And as I said earlier, my place may not be permanent even for me, but if you can hold off a little while, I'll give you a better answer."

"You set your play, then someone hikes the ball," Wiz says.

Momma looks confused.

Walter says, "He just means a lot of plans don't work out the way you expect."

"I promised Jack I'd give therapy a chance," Momma says. "That puts us on hold at least three months."

"We can keep him that long," Wiz says. "This is all on the QT, so we didn't lose our foster license over it. I'll be a stay-at-home foster dude for a bit. Shouldn't be any new surprises."

"No surprises except for maybe the smell," Walter says.

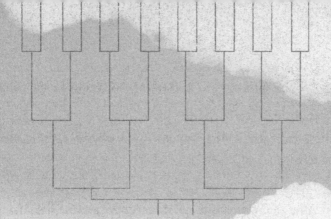

CHAPTER
SIXTEEN

Wiz says one of the scariest things about human beings is what slaves we are to habit. He did all the things needed to give Frankie a running start before he resigned, and then the ball got hiked, right around the time Sheila went into substance abuse treatment.

Margie was walking Sheila and Frankie down the long road toward reunification with great care and great love, way more than anyone's ever given her. Margie got her to agree that nothing good was going to happen until she was clean and sober, then placed her in inpatient treatment down in Yakima, where she could get away from all the people she's been dirty and messed-up with.

For a month she was in *blackout*: no visitors so she could focus on herself and her treatment. She got one phone call a week, which she didn't use because she didn't have anyone she wanted to call.

How pathetic is that?

After that month she still doesn't have anyone she's dying to talk to . . . so *my* phone goes off.

"Hey, Sheila."

"These assholes say I can have visitors now."

"That's great."

"Yeah," she says. "Great. Who would I want to see?"

"Me."

"Don't mess with me."

I say, "I'm not. You want to see me."

The line is quiet, then, "Okay. You."

On Saturday we don't have a game, and Leah had early workout. Tim is busy at home, so Leah and I make the three-hour drive to Yakima in two and a half. Leah scouts out coffee places where a girl can read for a couple hours while her BGF hangs out with her sister in drug treatment.

"So how is it?" I ask. We're in the main lounge, me in an overstuffed chair and her across the table on the couch.

"How do you *think*? It's drug treatment."

I am *not* doing battle. "Relatively speaking, then."

"Relatively to what? It's the only drug treatment place I've ever been in, if you haven't noticed."

I've noticed. "Sheila, I don't know how you want me to ask the question. Are you gonna make it?"

"My counselor says I'm doin' pretty good."

"That's great. How long do you think you're gonna be here?"

"I don't know," she says. "Of *course* I'm going good. I can't get my hands on anything."

"The brochure says you get individual and group counseling. Are you making any friends?"

"When have I ever had a friend?"

"Yvonne."

"Yvonne. I'm still pissed she told you where I was. I would never have texted. . . . "

"Come on. She was trying to help."

"An' she's like a weak little baby anyway. How is someone like Yvonne gonna help me through this? She uses as much as me, an' hell, I'd rather have *me* as a mother than her."

"I wasn't saying you should hook back up with Yvonne, even though *she* uses weed, and you use . . . whatever. I was saying if you can make one friend, you have the ability to make another, somebody who's, like, a little more together."

Sheila slaps the cushion. "This *couch* is more together than Yvonne."

I'm not helping. "So what do you want to talk about?"

"Tell me what's happening."

"Aren't you in touch with your caseworker?"

"No, I'm not in touch with my caseworker, other than she sends notes of 'support.' Bitch . . . get a job at Hallmark. Besides, when I wanna know what's really going on, I'm *not* askin' somebody who works for the state."

"Well," I say, "Frankie's still in at Wiz's place, waiting to see if the Howards are going to get it together as a permanent place."

"*I'm* a permanent place. What the hell do they think I'm doing in this shithole?" She says it loud and other patients glance over, then away when they catch Sheila's threatening look.

"You are a permanent place. But they have to have a fallback position in case you blow out."

She puts her head down, fiercely massaging the bridge of her nose. I don't know a whole lot about drug treatment, but Sheila's got a long way to go. If she got out of here today, she'd be flyin' by dinnertime.

"What about Ma?" she says.

"What about her?"

"You talk to her about all this? Me?"

"Little bit," I say. "You know Nancy. She blames it all on social services. When she's not blaming it on you."

"Yeah, well, I blame it on her."

I'm surprised she asked about Nancy at all.

She waits, then, "You think she'd come down here?"

"You mean to go into treatment?"

"No, dummy, to . . . do some sessions with me."

Wow.

"Somethin' they look for is resentments," Sheila says. "I got plenty of those. My counselor says it might be good if Ma came to a couple of sessions. Down the road, I mean."

I take a deep breath. "She *might*."

"Yeah, well, if you wanna make yourself useful, find out."

"She wants me to drive all the way down there and sit in a room with someone what's on her side so she can bash me?"

"That's not how she put it."

"A course that's not how she put it. You remember when *your* therapist roped me into coming in with you?"

"Uh-huh. Right after you brought a Level-three sex offender into our basement. 'He seems like a nice guy. I'll keep an eye on him.'" I'm wicked with the imitation.

We're in the mostly empty bleachers following a Friday night basketball game Nancy saw almost all of. Walter and Leah are about twenty yards away, each waiting to escort one of us home. Pop isn't here to criticize my play or keep me away from my family "lowlifes" because since he and Momma have been going to therapy, there's a moratorium on jumping my shit.

"Well," Nancy says, "I didn't bring no sex offenders down on your sister."

"I read the note the therapist gave her to give you. She's not bringing you there to get bashed. She wants to give Sheila the chance to get her feelings out and you the chance to respond."

"That's just a fancy way of sayin' I get one more chance to hear what a shitty mother I am."

I take a page from Seth's book. "Let me ask you a hypothetical question."

"You mean one that don't make sense."

"No. It's like a *what-if* question. If you knew that sitting through a few sessions would give Frankie a chance to live with his mother—like help him avoid what we all went through—would you do it?"

"You mean if I *knew* it would help?"

"Uh-huh."

She shakes her head as her shoulders slump. "I guess. But I got no way to get there."

"Leah and I'll take you. Walter can come, too, if he wants. We'll go to dinner after."

"Sounds like some miser'ble double date," she says.

"Exactly. A miserable double date, only Leah's boyfriend might take exception to that description."

I hear *intense* conversation through the heat-vent walkie-talkie in Marvin's room—Momma and Pop closed in their bedroom, wrestling over some therapy issue.

" . . . is not on the table, Jack. That girl has had more losses than any three kids should have had to suffer, and I'm *not* giving her one more."

"She lies," Pop says. "And then does whatever she pleases. I can't have that. What kind of message does that send to Marvin?"

"Jack, have you heard a *thing* we've talked about in therapy? And not that you've noticed, but Marvin is totally capable of deciphering all incoming messages. And you may *have* noticed he's so mad at you he can't see straight."

"A function of his immaturity."

"He *likes* Annie. And she likes him." It's quiet a minute, then, "You do realize, *dear*, that as long as Annie was lying about . . . *everything* she felt, you had no problem with her. It was when she started telling us who she really is that you came completely off the tracks."

"That's nonsense."

"You know, back in high school, this is the one thing my parents warned me about."

"Don't even start with your parents," Pop says. "Your father has always loved me like a son."

"My father likes you because he would do anything to make his daughter happy. You know what he said to me right after we told them we were getting married? He said, 'He's a good kid, Jane, but he has to have things his way. I hope you're ready for that.' And you know what? I thought I was. But you know what else? Over the years it's just made me sneaky."

I *feel* the air go tense. "Careful . . . " Then, "Have you had other relationships?"

"My *god* you are thick. No, I have not had other relationships. I've barely had this one, and if no other good comes from all of this, I am *finished* being careful."

I hear Pop's chair scoot, then, very low, in a total change of tone, "Jane, if I'm willing to work on *all* the other things that have come up, are you willing to give up Annie's placement here?"

"*All* the other issues?" Momma says.

I wish I could see their faces; Momma sounds interested, maybe even intrigued. My heart almost chokes me. I'm already out of Marvin's bedroom when Momma answers, because I do *not* want to hear it.

"You lose stuff from the day you're born," Walter says, "starting with a nice, warm safe place to be. You got to learn to lose it with grace, otherwise you leave no room for what's next. Learnin' that was the only way I come to manage everything the war took."

"How did you do it, Walter; or better how do *I* do it? She was . . . Momma said I didn't have to worry, and then, you should have heard her voice. I don't mind moving, but I couldn't stand her backing out on me. And it would mean no placement for Frankie . . . I couldn't stand to hear her tell Pop yes."

He shakes his head. "You hear Momma's voice through a heat grate and decide everything she's said to you up to now is a lie? That make sense? You're geared to believe folks are lying to you because of how you grew up. C'mon, girl, Jane Howard *loves* you, and you love her." He taps his temple. "*Think!*"

We're in our favorite corner at Revel, which is nearly empty in the early afternoon. "Some people pay a hundred fifty dollars for therapy, Walter. It only costs me a cup of coffee."

He laughs. "I was thinking of having a scone."

"You're covered, but we might have to extend the session."

"Slow day," he says. "I don't have another client until"—he looks at the wall clock—"well, hell, till you call again."

"You're probably right about Momma, but it's the

anticipation," I say. "It's not knowing for *sure*."

"Hate that," he says. "You know what I do about not knowing?"

"What?"

"I *know*—make the next thing happen," he says. "Why let somebody else decide your fate? Weigh in on your own. Let's say your cockamamie fear about Jane is real, which it is not. Tell the Howards to crap or get off the commode. Whaddaya got to lose? Hell, you're almost eighteen. In some cultures you'd be a sex slave by now."

He means I'd have a job.

"If anticipation is the enemy," he says, "kill it. Going up the losers bracket is the same in life as at Hoopfest. Lose one, kick 'er in gear. Basically we're talking about an education, right? The Howards were good for tuition?"

"Yeah, I mean they still might. And there's Marvin. I'd lose him, too."

"Tuition. Marvin. What the hell," he says. "They can't keep you from Marvin any more than they could keep you from your bios. And hell, do a couple years at community college—walk on if you can't get a scholarship—play hard, and get something at a four-year place."

"I don't know if I'm that good."

"Only one way to find out. If you don't stack up with the

big girls, go to a school with a crappy team. Plenty of those."

"Yeah, but . . . "

"Darlin'," he says, draining his coffee cup, "I can come up with solutions all day long and you can come up with reasons. Either you take control or all you've got left is reasons."

"Okay," I say. "Okay."

"Gonna sit here a while an' read," he says, hoisting his tattered book bag. "We still making that Yakima run?"

"Soon as I get the word from Sheila. Keep your calendar open."

I answer, "Come in," to the knock on my bedroom door.

"Hey, Annie," Momma says.

"Hey."

"Listen," she says, "we need to talk."

"Can I go first?"

"Of course."

"I think I should find another place to live."

"What?"

"It would make it a lot easier for you guys to figure things out."

She stands wide-eyed.

"I heard you talking. I know I'm, like, what Marvin calls the bargaining chip or something."

Momma rolls her eyes, takes a deep breath, and sits on the side of the bed. "No offense, but you'd be the lamest bargaining chip ever invented. You're not going anywhere. Or if you are, you're going with Marvin and me."

"I thought . . . "

"Annie, Jack's going to have to learn lessons he should have learned a long time ago. That, or I'll learn the *one* I need: that letting a man have his way all the time is the best way to turn him into an asshole. Look, Jack can be a nice guy, when he wants to be. He's funny, he makes a good living; compared to a lot of people, he might even be a passable parent. But I've let him tell me what's best for Marvin and you, and what's best for me, when I knew it was all best for *him*. I've always cajoled and danced and eventually gotten my way, but it's wearing me out."

"Yeah," I say, "but if I weren't here, you could just worry about your own family. Your relationship."

"You *are* my family. As snotty and bitchy as you can be, and you *can* be, you're ours, or mine. This isn't the first disagreement we've had about you."

"But still . . . "

"Enough. If I were to follow Jack's 'direction,' *or* if you were to leave because of all this uproar, I'd resent him for the rest of my life, or until I poisoned his soup." She stands. "Let us handle the big people's problems and you just get yourself through the rest of this year and figure out what's next. And you go see your family whenever you damn well please." She starts to walk out. "Just don't bring them here, except for Frankie, of course."

"But if Pop stays and I stay, he'll never talk to me."

"You can always hope," she says with a smile, and she's out the door.

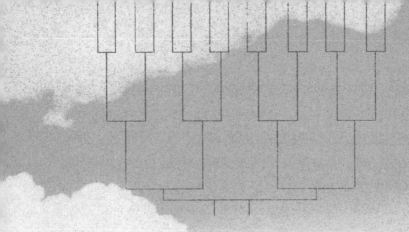

CHAPTER
SEVENTEEN

"This bitch better not start raggin' on me," Nancy says from the backseat as we turn off Interstate 90 at Ellensburg.

"Don't do that," Walter says. "You keep that in your head and anything she says will sound like ragging on you."

"Well, she just better not."

Having been in the system since I was a fetus, I'm pretty used to how therapy works. "It'll probably be like with that woman we used to see at the mental health center," I say. "The second one, Mary Ellen something. It's just a way to get everything out in the open."

"I don't want ever'thing out in the open. People been stickin' their nose in my life all of it. That's what happens when ever'thing is out in the open."

If I had the choice between being *this* therapist or Momma and Pop's, I'd choose suicide.

Walter says, "Nancy, you've told me how many times you wished you could do it all over. Nobody gets a chance to do *any* damn thing over, but once in a while we do get to make repairs."

"I don' know. This was just a bad idea."

I say, "You're just scared. Do you know how I used to hate it when you were coming into therapy with me? I was always afraid you were going to rat *me* out. Look, you'll be there an hour. You can take *any*thing for an hour. Can't be worse than the dentist. Then we go out on the town, stay in a nice place."

"Damn straight," Walter says. "'About time we classed this relationship up."

Leah's eyes are glued to the highway. This girl deserves a medal; she has *no* stake in any of this but agreed to drive so I didn't have to borrow Momma's car and get Pop all up in her face.

About ten miles outside Yakima, Leah takes a left into Re-Start's long driveway, then coasts into a small side parking lot.

"Y'all wait in the car," Walter says. "Or take a drive if you want. I'll be in the waiting room; I'll holler when they're done." He lifts his cell.

Walter and Nancy disappear through the front entrance and Leah drives around the circular drive. As she guns it, I see Walter waving in the rearview mirror. "Stop, Leah. We gotta go back."

"Gone," Walter says when we circle back.

"Where?" I ask.

Nancy stands on the concrete porch, stunned.

"Don't know," Walter says. "The woman in charge says some guy drove up and leaned on the horn. They called nine-one-one but Sheila ran out and jumped in. Left all her stuff." He takes Nancy by the arm and leads her to the backseat.

"Bitch," Nancy says. "Come all the way down here, ready to let 'er tear me up in front of one more damn counselor an' jus' like always. She runs."

When Leah pulls in front of Nancy's place that evening, we're spent. The *leisure* aspect of this trip crashed in unanimous agreement. Nearly four hours in the car, I'll bet we didn't say five words. Nancy sat in the backseat pissed and sad and dumb as she's ever been. Walter was smart enough to sleep. Leah drove and I stared out the window.

Walter gets out to open the door for Nancy, but she just bangs it open with her shoulder and stomps up her walk. He watches her go, looks for a second like he might follow, then gets back in the car. "Best drop me at my place," he says. "Let her cool down. There's no getting through that."

Momma and Pop were expecting me to stay in Yakima for the night, so Leah and I go to her house because everyone's out; she calls Tim and the three of us order pizza and watch a movie.

Maddy says, "This is a better story than most of the ones we read. What happens with Frankie?"

I have given the book club the *Reader's Digest* version of "The Ballad of Frankie Boots," with Leah filling in with an outsider's perspective, to great interest.

"He's with Wiz for now," I say, "but the plan is for Sheila to pull it together. More a *hope* than a plan, really."

Mark says, "It doesn't sound like your sister is coming to her senses anytime soon."

"I don't know that she has senses to come to," I say. "I should have remembered, just because Frankie aches for his mother doesn't mean she aches for him."

Leah says, "But remember, she came back after she disappeared and she also went to rehab; she had to have *some* connection to him. It was a dumb-ass plan to run, especially with all that gas I wasted. . . . "

I say, "Maybe she hates CPS more than she loves Frankie

and came back just to *show* them. Anyway, I don't know where it goes from here."

Seth's hand goes up. "I do believe we have come to the place where real life and literature separate."

I say, "Tell us, Seth."

"Editing," Seth says. "In literature, when circumstances don't play out well, the author rewrites. All the how-to writing books say it."

"And in real life . . . " Leah says, ushering Seth along.

"No rewrites. What's done is *done*."

"You guys know why I became a librarian?" Sharon asks.

Maddy says, "To increase the *hot* factor of all librarians throughout history?"

"There is that," Sharon says, "but . . . "

I remember. "*The Color Purple*."

"Beyond that," Sharon says.

"To hide your rack among the stacks?" Leah slaps her hand over her own mouth. "That just came out! It was like . . . bad rap!"

"That's what I get for asking a rhetorical question, right, Seth?" Sharon says, tapping her forehead. "I wanted to find the bridge between stories and life. As long as I can remember, every important literary character reminded me of someone, and almost all the ones I loved reminded me a little bit of me. Of course many of those I hated also reminded me of me. Seth is right; stories are . . . *cleaner*, because of rewrites. *We* don't get the rewrites, but we also don't have to bring our stories to conclusion in three hundred and fifty pages, so no rewrites, but do-overs, maybe."

Oliver says, "I like that."

"Something else has become clear to me," Sharon says, "listening to all your stories, and particularly this mess of Annie's. I think we've missed the boat, focusing on heroes and/or heroic acts; you know, finding them in fiction and then in life."

Leah says. "So what *should* we have been talking about?"

"Narrators," Sharon says. "The tellers of the tale. It isn't a question of whether or not you're the *hero* of your life, it's whether or not you're the narrator; whether you tell your own tale or let someone tell it for you. The characters I love stand up for themselves, understand that they run their own show."

I've heard this before in one form or another, from Leah and from Walter.

The conversation continues, but the rest is word salad to me because my mind slides down the road of "standing up for themselves. . . . " I see it again so clearly; I get so mad at Pop because *he* wants to tell *my* story. When he tries, I get devious and elusive; I lie, and live a story that's not his, but it's not mine, either. I felt such relief that evening in the den when I just gave up—refused to let him own me. So, easy enough: from here on out, tell the truth and let what happens, happen. The truth has a way of catching up to you, as they say, which sounds right, but I also need to catch up to *it*. But I'm on the other side of this, too. I want to control Nancy. I've done everything to make her feel guilty about not taking care of me in the first place and about not keeping contact. I want to control Sheila, because I want to control what happens to Frankie. Maybe Sharon is right. Maybe those aren't my stories.

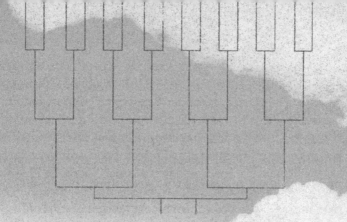

CHAPTER
EIGHTEEN

It's crazy how things work, or maybe how they don't. As much time as we've spent in book club talking about books we've read and the "lessons" that come out of them and as much time as I've spent with Walter, who's like some kind of guru, I don't know any more about how life works than I did when I was five. I remember talking with Mark about God one night after book club last year, walking away thinking *I hope he's right.* I hoped some great big entity is watching, some entity who wants things to turn out right . . . and who has the power to make that happen. But at the same time I was afraid to want it, because of how much it hurts to not get it. When I was five, I was back with Nancy and Sheila for a fairly extended period, one that ran through the Christmas holidays. Nancy was using again, just hadn't been caught, and Rance was in and out for some reason that probably had to do with dealing. Sheila had taken over what parenting duties there were, even though she was barely a year and a half older than me, and we'd been downtown looking in store windows. She kept asking me what I wanted for Christmas and I picked some things out. She told me I had to ask Santa Claus *real nice* and if I'd been good, I'd get them. Christmas was only a week or so away, and I remember thinking I hadn't been all that good or I wouldn't keep having to go away, but if I could do everything right for a week, Santa might come with the goods.

And I was *so* good. I didn't cry or call names, and was seriously obedient . . . helped Nancy steal groceries and hid money under my bed that she'd snuck out of Rance's billfold. When I woke up on Christmas morning I didn't get anything I wanted; in fact, I didn't get anything. First day back at kindergarten our teacher asked about our vacations, and it seemed like every kid got at least one thing they asked for. I couldn't believe I was the worst kid in the class, but the jury was in. I can't tell you how glad I was to find out later that there wasn't a Santa Claus.

So as much as I wanted to believe in the God Mark talked

about, I was just too afraid to wake up and find out I haven't been good enough.

Things do get on a roll and a hand may be guiding them, but not necessarily a good one.

A few days after Sheila disappeared from drug treatment, Frankie disappeared again . . . right from Wiz's place. Wiz was in town at the library and his wife had put Frankie to bed. When Wiz got home and stuck his head in Frankie's room, the bed was empty. They didn't think much of it; Frankie is famous for wandering in the night, but they scoured the house and Frankie was gone. Wiz called 911, then alerted everyone who even knew Frankie's name. Pop and Momma forgot their differences and jumped in the car and I texted Leah, who was out with Tim, and they were at my place in minutes.

I jump in the backseat and Leah says, "Yvonne's."

I say, "What?"

"It's gotta be your sister. Frankie wasn't in the park this time; he was home in bed. That's not a stranger."

"Yvonne's," I say, and Leah barks the directions at Tim.

"Yvonne, when was the last time you saw Sheila?"

"Couple of days ago, I guess." Yvonne is cross-legged on her couch, smoking a joint—candles lit all over the place, low music floating in from another room. No wonder she wasn't startled when Leah and I found the door unlocked and stormed in.

"What was she like, I mean, her attitude? Did she say anything crazy?"

Yvonne shakes her head slowly. "Said she was done. Had enough. No more."

"Enough of what?" Leah asks. "Did she say what she was going to do?"

"Nope. Just done, is all. She told me I was a 'weak, worthless bitch' an' she was done with me, too. I think she was on something, but I also think she meant it."

I say, "Nothing about Frankie, or where she was going?"

"Nope. Think she has a new girlfriend, though. How do you like that? I do everything to steer her away from all the assholes, and she picks another chick."

"A *girl*friend? That doesn't sound right. Are you sure?"

"Yeah, some bitch named . . . Susan or something."

Shit! I push Leah out the door, where Tim waits on the porch. "Do you know Badger Lake?"

Tim says, "I've heard of it."

"It's where we swam open water practicing for the Sandpoint swim," Leah tells him. "Out past Turnbull."

Tim says, "Right."

I say, "We gotta get there fast."

We're in the car, shooting through neighborhood streets like Tim's a NASCAR driver; we hit Ash, cross the Maple Street bridge, and shoot west onto the freeway in what has to be record time.

Leah says, "Who's this Susan? The new girlfriend?"

"Susan isn't a real person . . . at least not real to Sheila," I say. "She was talking about Susan Smith."

"The woman that . . . "

"Yup."

Leah punches Tim's arm. "Hurry, baby. *Hurry!*"

I tell Siri to call Wiz; I can barely think. He'll know what else to do and *maybe* he'll calm me down.

He picks up on the first ring. "Hey, Annie."

"I think Sheila's got him, and I think we're in trouble. I'm with Leah. We just talked to Yvonne, and I think Sheila's headed out to Badger Lake."

"Where is Badger Lake?"

"Out past the Turnbull wildlife refuge," I say. "Sheila said something to Yvonne about Susan Smith."

"Susan Smith?" he says. "The woman who . . . "

" . . . drowned her kids," I say. "She's mentioned her before; Sheila and I were out at Badger once, right after the first time she thought you guys were going to take Frankie.

There's a little resort, and we were sunbathing on the dock next to the boat launch. Sheila said if you guys ever tried to take Frankie, she'd do a Susan Smith. We fought over it; she finally said she wasn't serious, but now . . . I don't know. For some reason that boat launch reminded her . . . "

"Jesus."

"Yeah, listen," I say, "can you call nine-one-one in Cheney? We're close, but they can probably get there faster. I mean, she *could* be going to some other lake, but she's pretty literal, it's all I can think of."

"If she's got him," Wiz says, "she took him from *here* and we're close to a huge lake with hundreds of private boat launches. *You* call Cheney nine-one-one and I'll get them on Amber Alert. You cover Badger; I'll alert the Coeur d'Alene police."

I click off and hit 911.

A quicker way to get the Cheney police on the move is to drive down an almost deserted Main Street at seventy miles per hour, which is exactly what Tim does. The Cheney cop comes after us and Tim puts the pedal to the floor, while I'm talking to 911 telling them why we're breaking the law and all speeding records. The dispatcher tells me to stay on the line while she alerts the officer on our tail, and gets up with the state police. On one hand I think this is a long shot, and on another I think I *have* to be right. *Please* let there be *some* hand in the universe that cares more about Frankie than Santa Claus.

As Tim turns onto the Badger Lake road we start into a skid, but he pulls it out and actually speeds up.

The park on the lake is nearly empty; summer is long past. Dim lights glow from the windows of the few trailers inhabited by folks who live here year-round, but the grounds are mostly dark. We jump out, frantically searching for the public launch as the Cheney policeman rolls in behind us, but for the life of me I can't get my bearings.

"The public launch!" Tim yells. "Where is it?"

I whirl in a three-sixty, but nothing looks familiar. It was summer when we were here, daylight. There were boats. . . .

Leah sprints to an oversized camper, pounds on the door, and begs for directions. She comes running, pointing and yelling, "Behind the blue camper!

And there they are, two taillights glowing beneath the surface, not deep, but fully submerged. Bubbles rise to the surface.

Tim kicks off his shoes as he sheds his coat and outer shirt and hits the water on the shotgun side, Leah seconds behind him on the other. Tim surfaces, yelling, "Air pocket! A rock! Anything hard! Quick!"

I scramble, picking up and discarding possible weapons, till I find a rusty tire iron next to a boat trailer and run into the water to Tim. Leah goes under on the other side with a rock, while I bang on the trunk lock with a too-small piece of concrete I found lying next to the dock.

The Cheney cop is shouting directions into his radio while Tim and Leah bash in windows, and my hunk of concrete disintegrates in my hands.

"Got him!" Tim yells, and pulls a drenched five-year-old up the ramp, lays his body on the dock, puts an ear to Frankie's mouth . . . then, "They haven't been down long. He's breathing."

Leah yells from the other side, dragging Sheila's still form onto the sand beside the dock. "Sheila's *not*!" She turns her over, strikes her hard between the shoulder blades, and Sheila coughs.

Tim yells, "Get the kid in the car, heat on *high*," and I grab Frankie, while Tim rushes to help Leah.

April 22— Session #Who's Counting?
ANNIE BOOTS

Came in relaxed; jeans and a very nice blouse; appears more "feminine" than usual, though that could be therapist bias. Seemed more "open."

Annie: So, counselor lady, this is it, huh?

Me: For now.

Annie: What's that mean?

Me: The door's always open, Annie. For you.

Annie: Aren't you going to fill my spot?

Me: You mean with some other eight-year-old beastie; hopeless half the time and weaponized the other half?

Annie: (laughs) Was I that bad?

Me: Let's just say you were first. I was new to the game. And yeah, I'll fill your spot, but when things come up . . . you've got my number. So how do you want to use this time?

Annie: You know how I always ask you for advice and you almost never give it . . . you ask questions till I come up with the advice you'd have given me anyway?

Me: Busted.

Annie: I want to ask the questions today.

Me. Last day. I guess I can bend my style.

Annie: And you can't answer any of my questions with one of your own.

Me: Busted again. Fire away.

Annie: Am I going to make it?

Me: Yes.

Annie: How do you know?

Me: You've already gone through the tough stuff, and here you are.

Annie: But am I going to make it?

Me: (handing her the envelope I intended to give her at the end of the session) I have one full file drawer of notes on you. It's been a real ride. I'm giving you these few from this year so you can read them and remind yourself what you know.

Annie: Want me to read them now?

Me: No.

Annie: So, my question.

Me: Of course it depends on your definition of "making it." I think you're always going to be conflicted, and you're always going to have to watch your temper. I think you're going to have to be very careful who you decide to share your life with, and who you decide to let into your life in general . . . you know, friends. You've told me a number of times that my office is the only place where you tell the whole truth. I would suggest that you look for those few people out in the world you're willing to take a chance on. And then take it.

Annie: I don't know. . . .

Me: I'd start with your friend, Leah. Maybe Walter. And you're going to meet a whole new bunch of possibilities when you start college.

Annie. I'm scared.

Me: Good.

Impression: I break out the farewell cake, and we pig out.

Emily Palmer, M.A.

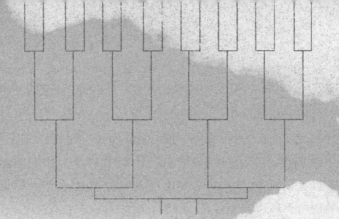

CHAPTER
NINETEEN

Thanksgiving: The following year

I back into a parking spot in the strip mall across the street from Quik Mart and kill the engine; Momma helped me buy this clean-but-well-used Chevy after graduation. This will be a catch-up day with my bios. I've had no lengthy conversations with them, haven't run into them on the street, something that would have made Pop happy if he still lived with us. These days it's me and Marvin and Momma, and the unsinkable Frankie Boots.

I finished my senior basketball season strong but not like a superstar, and got a couple partial scholarship offers. Momma said she'd cover the balance, but she's only exactly half as well-to-do as when she was with Pop, and I don't want to be cutting into Marvin's education trust—little shit will be Ivy League. Or Stanford. At any rate. I opted to take that job at the multiplex and play at least a year at community college to see if I can up my stock with a Division II school, just like Walter advised.

So far this preseason, I haven't dazzled the coaches. My heart isn't quite Michael Jordan yet.

I'm watching the side entrance to Quik Mart—don't want to get there first—and haven't seen anyone else go in, so I lower my seatback, plug my iPhone into the radio, and kick back to my playlist for this month. This is the first Boots Thanksgiving Day Ritual Dinner I won't have to sneak to. I invited the book club, but after I described it . . . no takers. Leah said, "Annie girl, I'll know your mind is right when you *skip* that fiasco!" Oscar said it sounded like a pretty horrible thing to do to an immigrant. Seth said it sounded like an affront to Indians and Pilgrims alike.

Sitting here waiting for people, some of whose bloodstream I share, I can't help but float back to what brought me here.

I still meet with Walter at Revel at least once a week; I'm glad he never stopped following me. When I finally digested that night we chased down Frankie, I guess I truly came to terms with how crazy my life has been and it's been almost lifesaving to have a place to talk about it.

I look through my windshield now to see Sheila walking into Quik Mart, resplendent in her government-issue orange jumpsuit, which she's wearing by *choice* ("Be proud of who you are."), holding Frankie's hand. The woman close behind them is the visitation supervisor. No unsupervised visits for the incarcerated, whether or not you're clean and sober.

In less than a minute, Nancy appears from the other side of the building; Rance following like a dutiful puppy. Gotta wonder how he tricked her into an invite.

And then Wiz and his wife, Rachel. Before this day is done *she'll* wish she'd gone ahead and cooked Thanksgiving dinner at home, but now that Wiz is "starting over," he wants "new experiences." We'll see.

Walter steps out of a taxi, scans the premises till he sees me parked across the street. He waves. "Annie! Get over here!"

We hug on the walkway next to the gas pumps. "Sure you're up for this?" I ask.

"Up for it?" he says. "I'm footin' the bill."

"There are a lot more people here than usual."

Walter just shrugs.

"We better go in," I say, "before Nancy starts taking her five-finger discount. She's wearing her Walmart dress. It *might* be a coincidence, but she's hardwired, I'm afraid."

"Indeed she is," he says, and opens the door for me.

Inside, Boots and friends take over the small sitting area back near the restrooms, where city workers and clerks on lunch break from the strip mall usually sit to grab a quick sandwich.

But this has been going on for years, and on Thanksgiving Day that area is roped off for the Boots. To make it financially worthwhile for Quik Mart, tradition says no one brings anything in; the entire dinner is purchased on site: turkey burgers and dogs, olives and potato and macaroni salads from the mini-deli that may or may not carry E. coli.

Though Quik Mart sells wine, you're not allowed to drink on the premises, so Walter buys a few bottles and hides them in the toilet tank in each restroom, where you sneak in to fill the Diet Pepsi can you brought inside your backpack, or in Nancy's case, under her billowing dress. Since it's illegal to drink it here anyway, age doesn't matter. Except for Frankie, of course. *No*body want to see *that* little bugger drunk.

Walter leaves his credit card in the care of Nellie Mae Britain, who has drawn cashier duty for this prestigious event as far back as I can remember. She works here full-time but no matter how the shift schedule is drawn up, Nellie Mae oversees the Bootses' ode to the Mayflower. Back in the day,

I'd sneak over here after regular Thanksgiving dinner at the Howards; they could never understand why I ate so little on the one day you're allowed to stuff yourself till you pop. I'd say I had to go visit a friend or see a movie, or just fall ill so I could go to my room, then pop out my bedroom window and come eat myself comatose on premium Quik Mart fare, all purchased at wholesale plus three percent.

"Ladies and gentlemen!" Nancy stands at what she considers to be the head of the table. The tables are identical round wire mesh, pushed together and covered with butcher paper, but on Thanksgiving, wherever the big momma lands is the head of the table.

"Welcome," she booms. "Another year, another recognition a' the power of family. So good to see ever'body here. 'Cept maybe for Rance. Getting rid of him is like scrapin' a turd off the bottom of yur shoe on a hot day." No matter what decency lurks beneath, my mother cannot shake her sense that empowerment occurs only when she's standing on someone's neck.

Rance smiles and nods like he's been given an award. Wonder what *he's* on.

"Got a lot to be thankful for this year," she goes on, "'sides the Pilgrims and Indians who probably didn't like each other anyway. Like to interduce a few people, case you end up sittin' next to one of 'em and don't know what to say. This year for the first time we got a social worker in our midst, maybe the only one in the history of social workers ain't a devil. Wiz, you wanna raise yur hand?"

Wiz raises his hand. "Ex-social worker," he says.

"Best kind. I suppose that hot thing next to you is your lovely wife. Don't think I know her name. How'd you land such a thing? You ain't what most of us would call a catch. 'Course what am *I* talkin' about? My ol' man ain't exactly The Rock. Walter, stick your hand up."

In Nancy's world, that passes for comedy. Walter closes his eyes and raises his hand.

"My daughter's here. Big college athlete—didn't know if she'd show this year. Haven't seen much of her lately, what with her gettin' all that fancy education, but I guess there are some things so rooted in your history you just can't stay away. Stand up, Annie."

I stand and take a bow. "I've been looking forward to it since Halloween, Nancy."

"I'll bet. 'Course there's my other daughter. Now there's somethin' to be thankful for. Looks like there's a perty good chance this third time through drug treatment might take— long as they keep her in prison—an' next thing you know her little poop pusher will be livin' with her and her friend

Yvonne, who's spent the last four years or so turnin' her into one of them chicks who do chicks. Wanna stand up an' take a bow, Yvonne?"

Yvonne just stares at the butcher paper.

"Hey, I'm behind ya all the way," Nancy says. "Sheila's got the kinda taste in *men* that should make her wanna drink about a gallon of Listerine." She clasps her hands together. "So," she says, "it's another Thanksgiving which means we got to bow our heads and pump out a little grace. Sheila, since your givin' us the most to be thankful for, why don't you lead us in prayer."

Without hesitation Sheila takes Frankie's hand on one side and Yvonne's on the other, bows her head, and says, "Sweet Jesus, thanks for shutting my fat mother up so we can finally eat. Amen."

In my family, that kind of patter passes for endearment.

To fully appreciate this spectacle, you have to remember that Quik Mart hasn't closed its doors to host this Boots jamboree. Through it all, folks are coming in to pay for gas or grab a couple of forgotten items for their own celebrations and I swear, *to the person*, they look at us like they took a wrong turn off the main road and couldn't find a turnaround until they'd gone so far up the holler they hit a time warp.

So we eat.

Halfway through the meal, in walks Marvin. He waves at me from the door and says, "You guys really have this! I thought it was an urban legend." He gives Walter a quick fist-bump, ruffles Frankie's hair, and squeezes in next to me. "I gotta have at least one turkey dog," he says, "just so I can say I had the experience. Who's got a phone? I *must* chronicle this in my history."

I've only taken a small bite out of *my* poultry surprise—my third—so I hand it over. He squeezes in a couple of packets of relish and some mayo and finishes it in three bites. "Man," he says, "this is, like, epic."

"Remember," I tell him, "what you 'chronicle in your history' can also be used as evidence."

When we're almost finished, Leah and Tim show. I leap up and run to hug them, while Sheila turns her back. When Sheila was still in the hospital, under guard even, Leah got in to see her, only to hear Sheila chastise her for pulling her out of the car. Sheila seems happier to be alive now, so the turning away is likely embarrassment.

Right now, Leah says, "So this is *real*."

I say, "If you can call it that. You guys want something to eat?"

Tim looks around with great skepticism, pats his stomach, and says, "Love to, but I'm in training."

Leah laughs. "We're here for dessert."

"Two ice cream sandwiches coming up." Walter has snuck in behind us.

I stand in the middle of Quik Mart between two of the fastest—and culturally unlikeliest—swimmers in the state of Washington, grateful that Momma Jane has tethered me to her, so I feel safe surveying those to whom I am connected by biology and the flow of time. They've ravaged one another and me, and I've ravaged them back. We've turned our backs on one another a thousand times, only to turn again into reluctant embrace. They're so unhinged they can kill, but so far they haven't—thanks to a lead-footed Korean breaststroker who swims distance freestyle and his kickass girlfriend . . . and a lot of luck. Bill Bryson tells us in *A Short History of Nearly Everything* that advances in evolution are very often accomplished not so much through the overpowering superiority of one species over another, but through certain unique mutations of the ordinary, slipping through a rapidly closing window and building on those mutations. It may be arrogant, but I think of myself as the Boots kid who slipped through that window. I'm the first of my clan to graduate high school and get into community college, and though it's not WSU or the U-Dub, don't count me out; I'd look good in a Cougars or Huskies jersey.

It would be easy to lay my relative good fortune at the feet of Momma and Marvin and even Pop; they certainly provided stability and lots of second chances. But—and this might seem like a hard case to make—I also stand on the shoulders of the Bootses. There probably won't be a time in the foreseeable future when I can give a money-back guarantee that my next encounter with Nancy or Sheila or even Rance will be skirmish free. None of us would have struggled like this if there hadn't been some glue—some love, or connection, or whatever—and I have to admit that the part of me that hangs on like a pit bull has saved me as many times as it's shamed me. So here I sit, watching Marvin polish off another turkey dog to the tune of Nancy's irreverent verbal bombs, my sister in orange and my bio dad in a coma, and I have to give us kudos. I mean, hell, we're still standing.

↩ ↩ ↩